IN THE TIME BEFORE TIME,
THERE WAS NOTHING, KAOS.

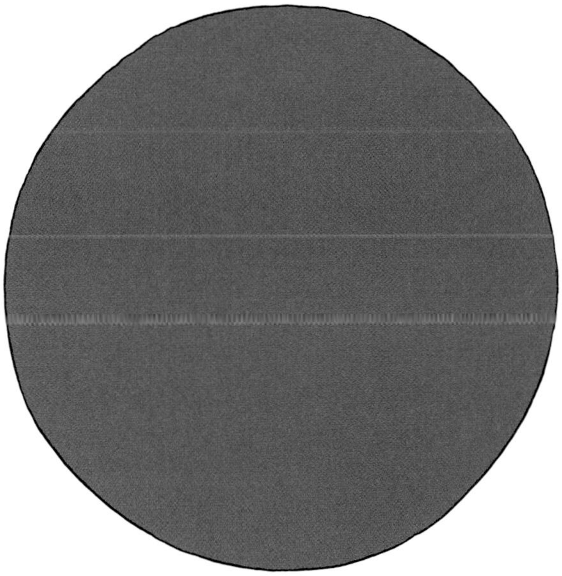

FROM OUT OF KAOS CAME GE,
OR GAEA, OUR MOTHER EARTH.

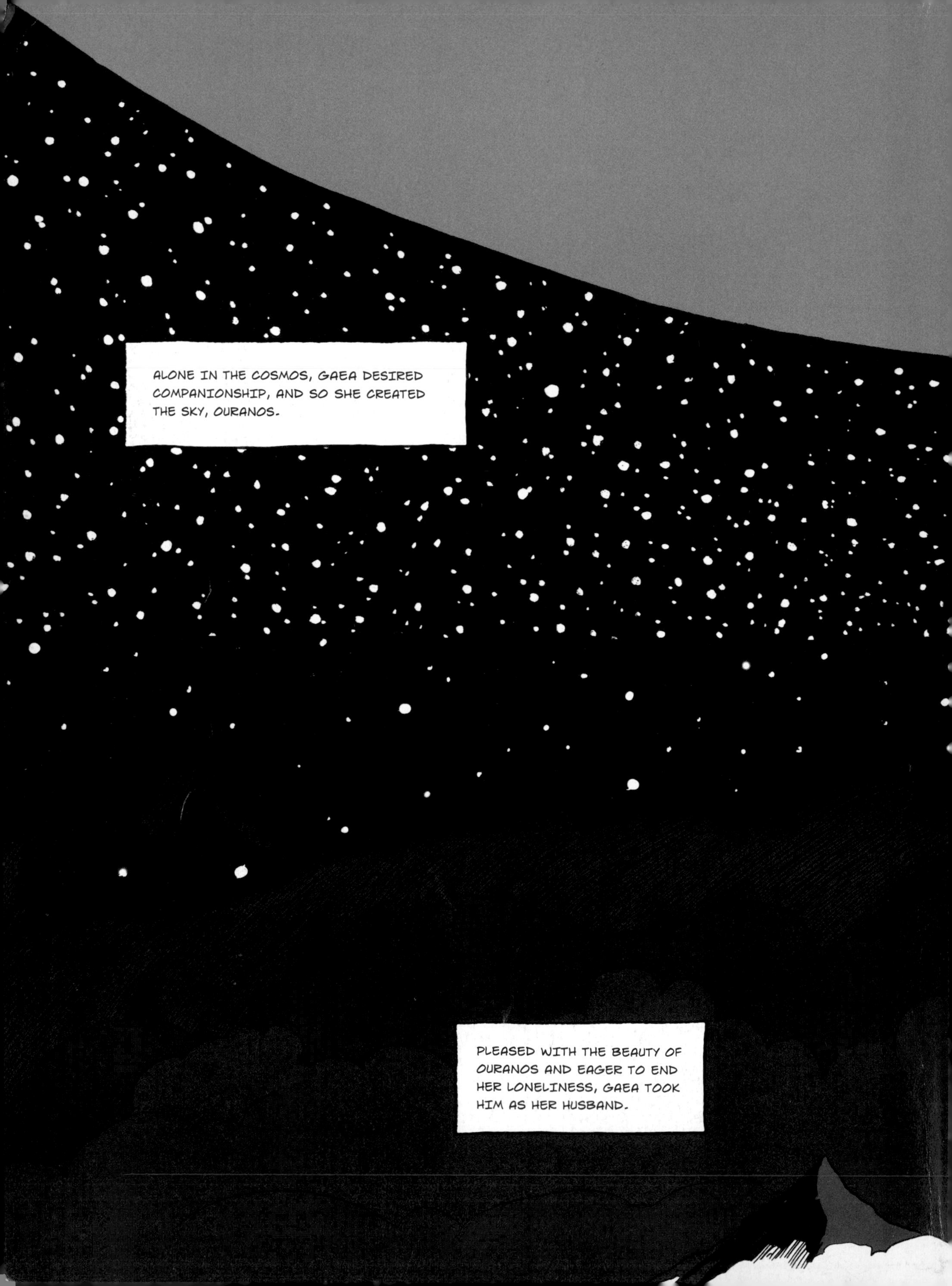
ALONE IN THE COSMOS, GAEA DESIRED COMPANIONSHIP, AND SO SHE CREATED THE SKY, OURANOS.
PLEASED WITH THE BEAUTY OF OURANOS AND EAGER TO END HER LONELINESS, GAEA TOOK HIM AS HER HUSBAND.

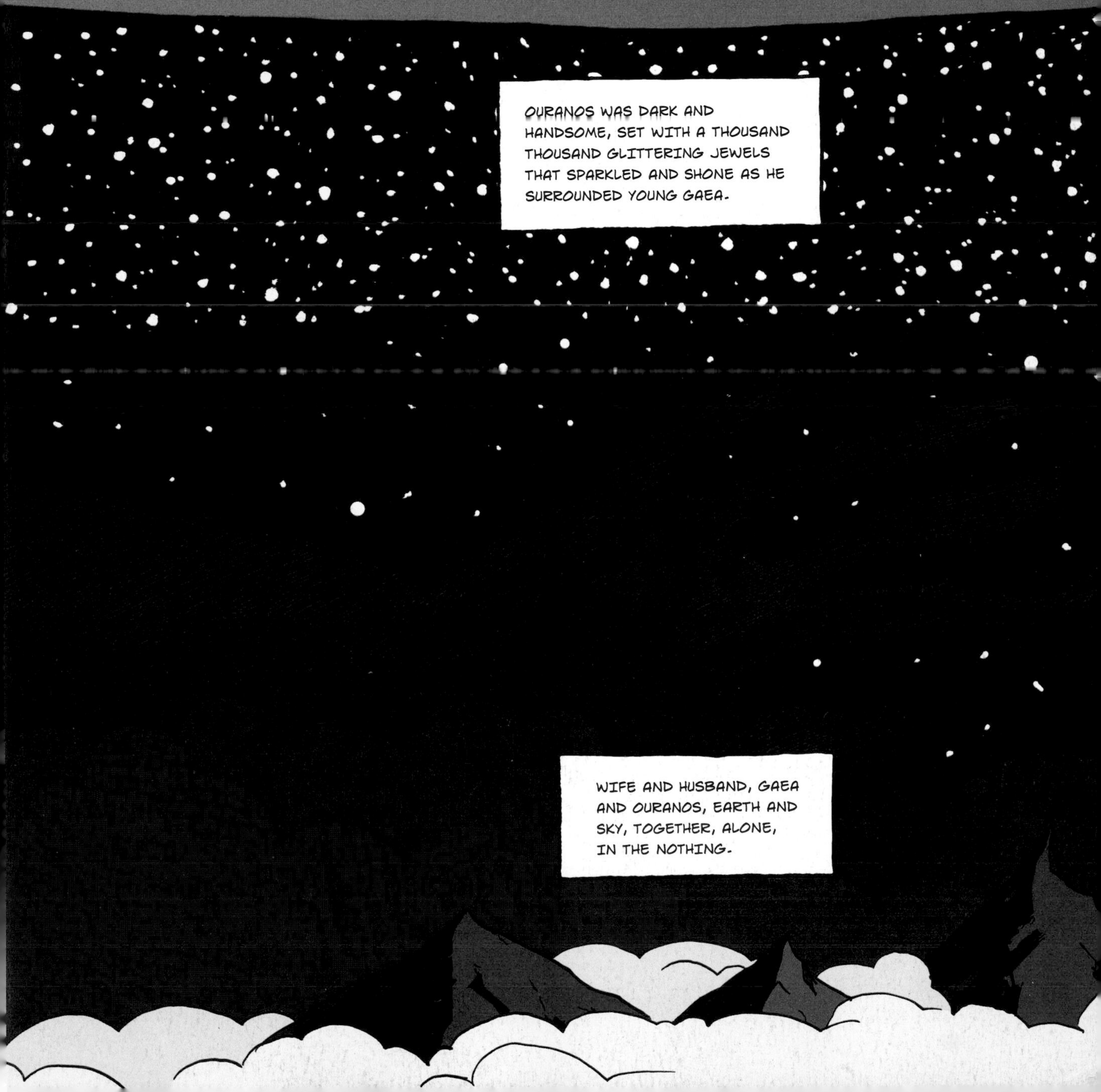
OURANOS WAS DARK AND HANDSOME, SET WITH A THOUSAND THOUSAND GLITTERING JEWELS THAT SPARKLED AND SHONE AS HE SURROUNDED YOUNG GAEA.
WIFE AND HUSBAND, GAEA AND OURANOS, EARTH AND SKY, TOGETHER, ALONE, IN THE NOTHING.

THIS WAS NOT TO LAST. WITH THE CREATION OF OURANOS, THERE WAS CHANGE, AND WITH THE BEGINNING OF CHANGE, TIME.

AND, IN TIME, GAEA BECAME PREGNANT.

THE FIRST CHILDREN OF EARTH AND SKY WERE THE GODS OF TIME.

THE TITANS WERE NOT THE ONLY CHILDREN OF GAEA AND OURANOS.

THERE WERE THE THREE CYCLOPES, ENORMOUS AND POWERFUL AS STORMS, EACH POSSESSED OF ONLY ONE GLOWING EYE.

AND THE THREE HEKA-TONCHIERES, EACH OF THEM WITH FIFTY HEADS AND ONE HUNDRED HANDS.

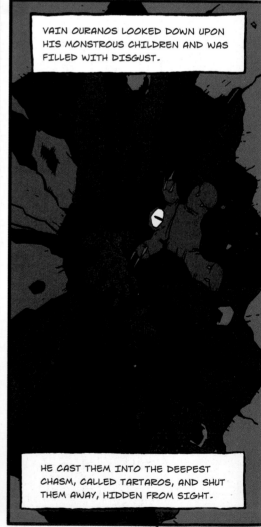

VAIN OURANOS LOOKED DOWN UPON HIS MONSTROUS CHILDREN AND WAS FILLED WITH DISGUST.

HE CAST THEM INTO THE DEEPEST CHASM, CALLED TARTAROS, AND SHUT THEM AWAY, HIDDEN FROM SIGHT.

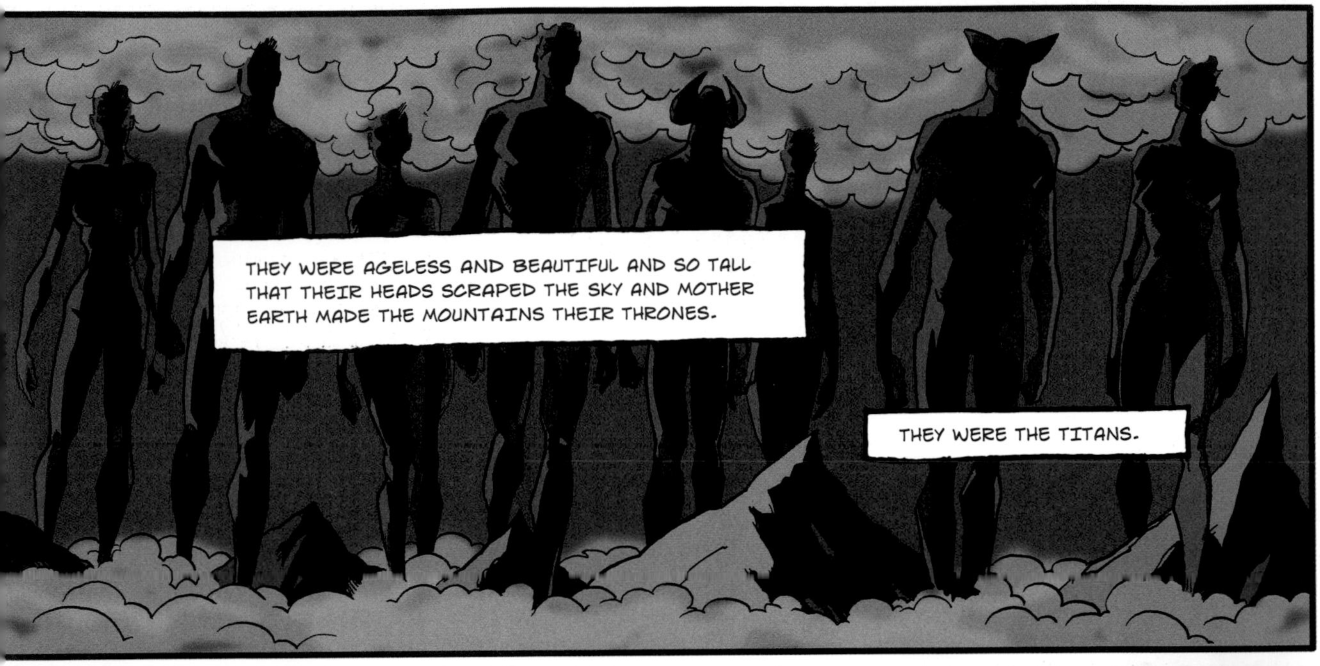
THEY WERE AGELESS AND BEAUTIFUL AND SO TALL THAT THEIR HEADS SCRAPED THE SKY AND MOTHER EARTH MADE THE MOUNTAINS THEIR THRONES.
THEY WERE THE TITANS.

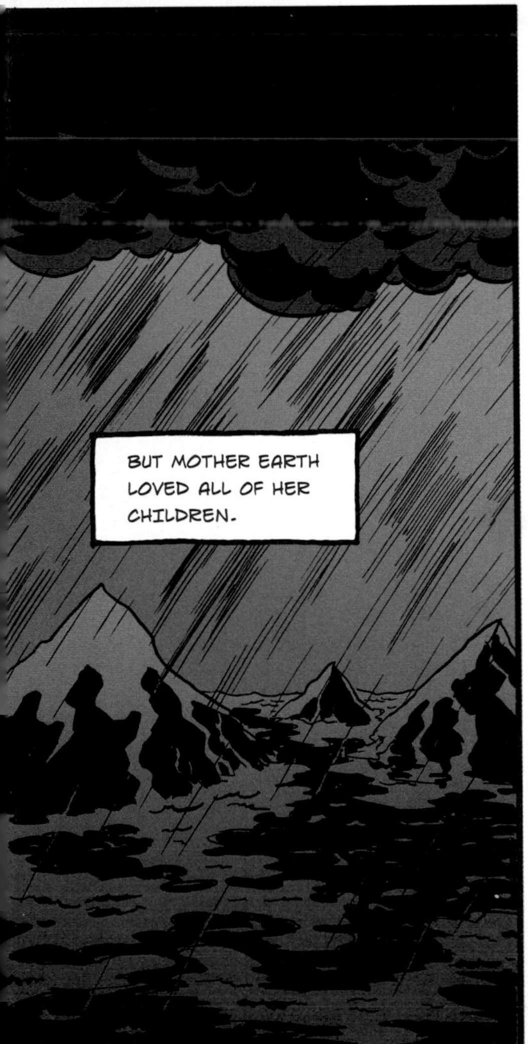
BUT MOTHER EARTH LOVED ALL OF HER CHILDREN.

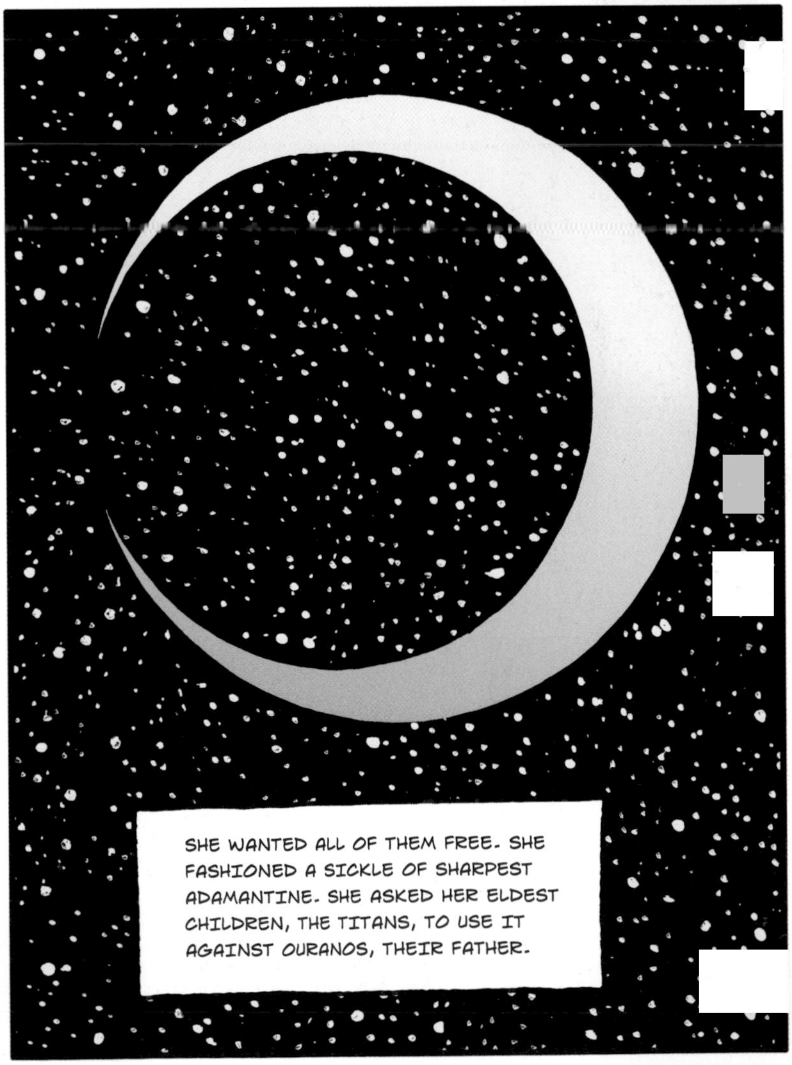
SHE WANTED ALL OF THEM FREE. SHE FASHIONED A SICKLE OF SHARPEST ADAMANTINE. SHE ASKED HER ELDEST CHILDREN, THE TITANS, TO USE IT AGAINST OURANOS, THEIR FATHER.

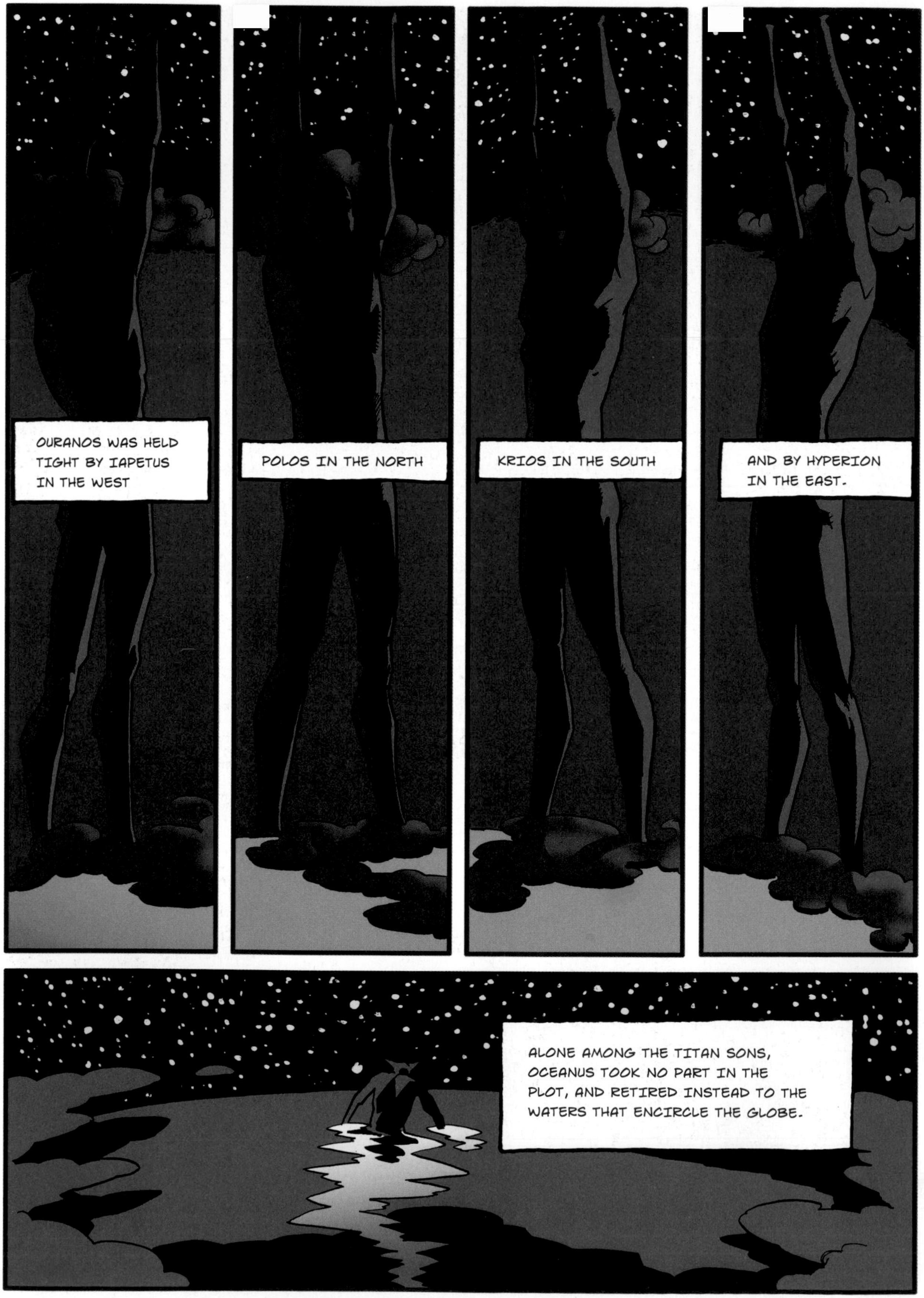
OURANOS WAS HELD TIGHT BY IAPETUS IN THE WEST
POLOS IN THE NORTH
KRIOS IN THE SOUTH
AND BY HYPERION IN THE EAST.
ALONE AMONG THE TITAN SONS, OCEANUS TOOK NO PART IN THE PLOT, AND RETIRED INSTEAD TO THE WATERS THAT ENCIRCLE THE GLOBE.

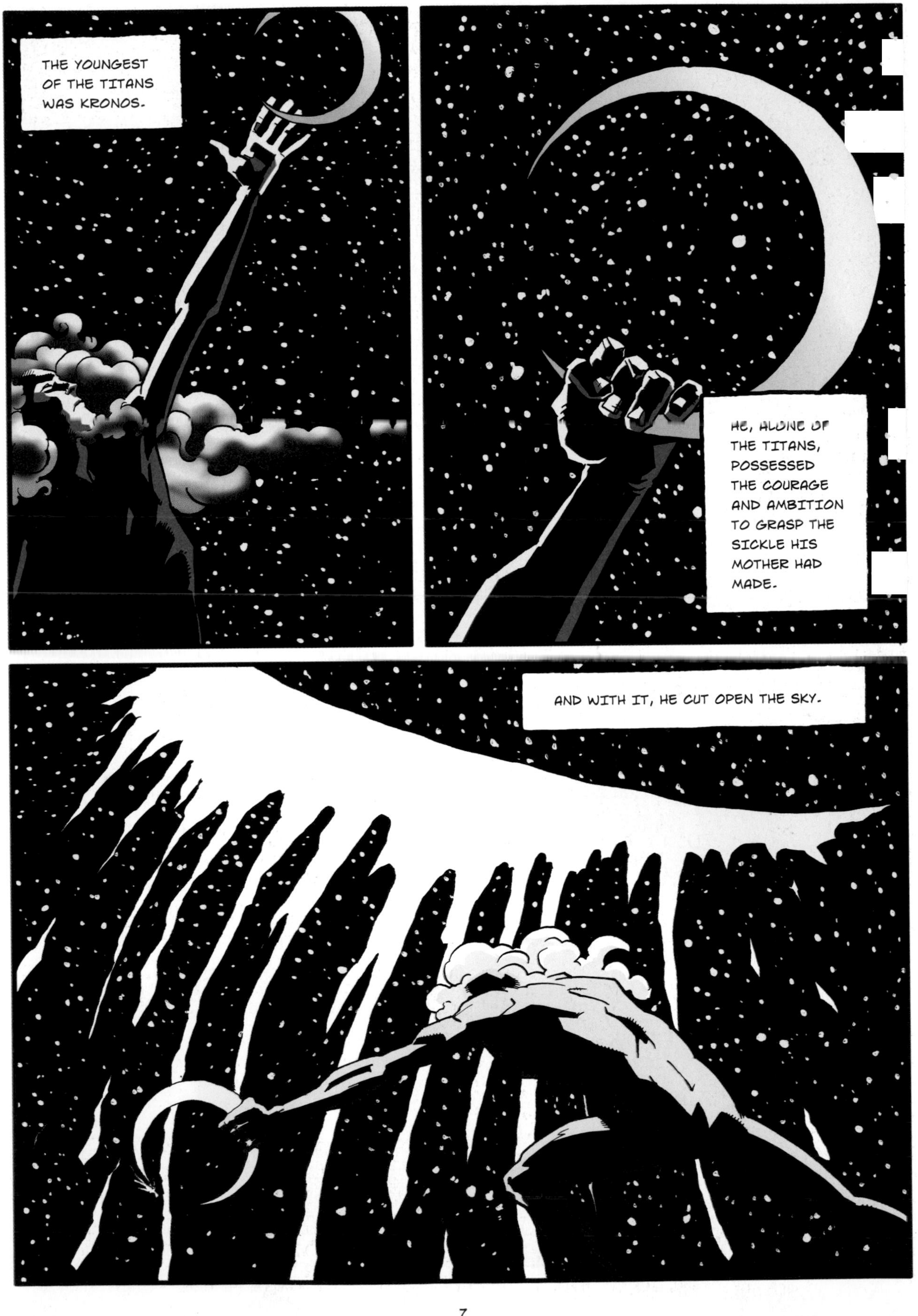
THE YOUNGEST OF THE TITANS WAS KRONOS.
HE, ALONE OF THE TITANS, POSSESSED THE COURAGE AND AMBITION TO GRASP THE SICKLE HIS MOTHER HAD MADE.
AND WITH IT, HE CUT OPEN THE SKY.

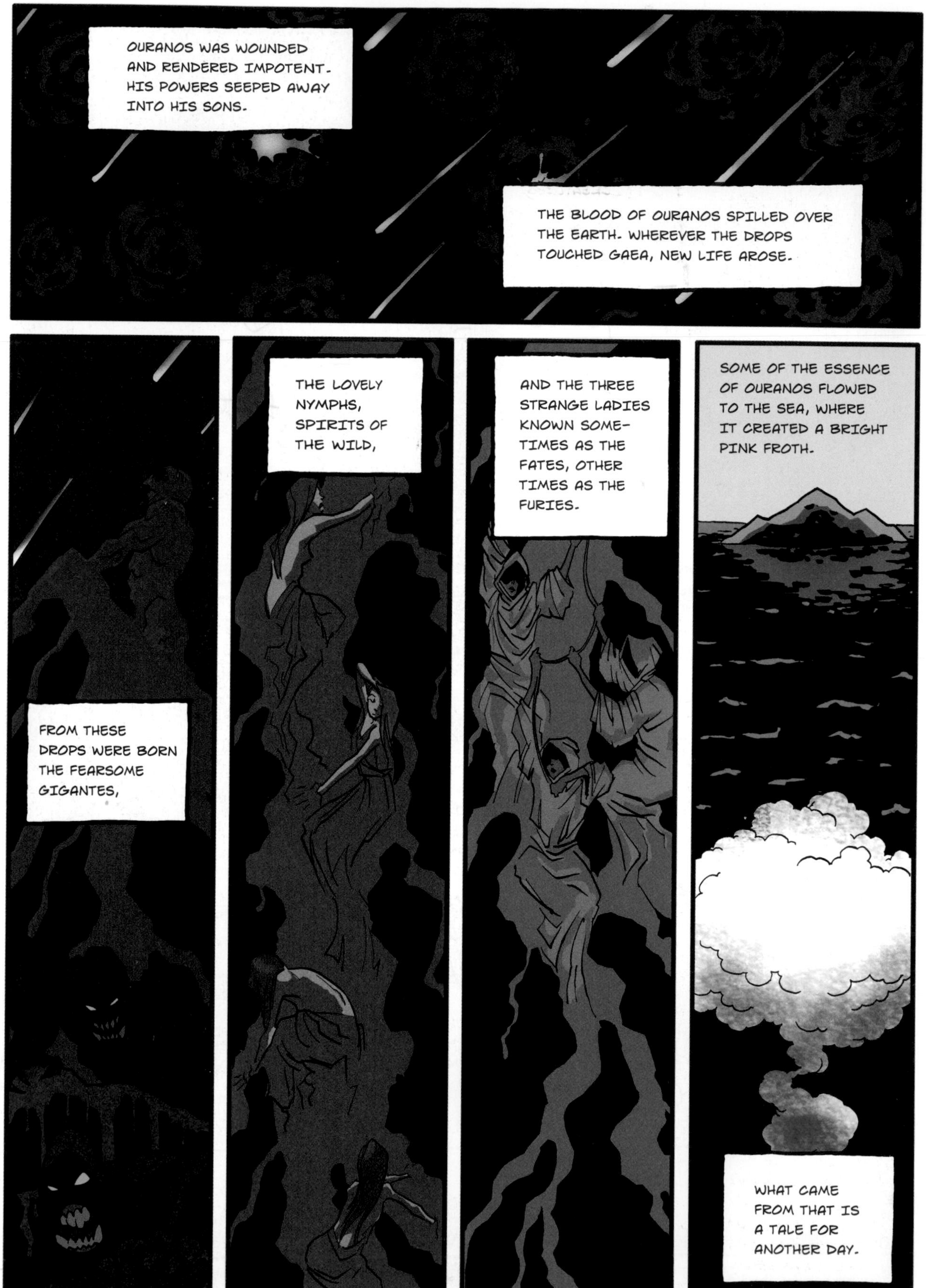
OURANOS WAS WOUNDED AND RENDERED IMPOTENT. HIS POWERS SEEPED AWAY INTO HIS SONS.
THE BLOOD OF OURANOS SPILLED OVER THE EARTH. WHEREVER THE DROPS TOUCHED GAEA, NEW LIFE AROSE.
FROM THESE DROPS WERE BORN THE FEARSOME GIGANTES,
THE LOVELY NYMPHS, SPIRITS OF THE WILD,
AND THE THREE STRANGE LADIES KNOWN SOME-TIMES AS THE FATES, OTHER TIMES AS THE FURIES.
SOME OF THE ESSENCE OF OURANOS FLOWED TO THE SEA, WHERE IT CREATED A BRIGHT PINK FROTH.
WHAT CAME FROM THAT IS A TALE FOR ANOTHER DAY.

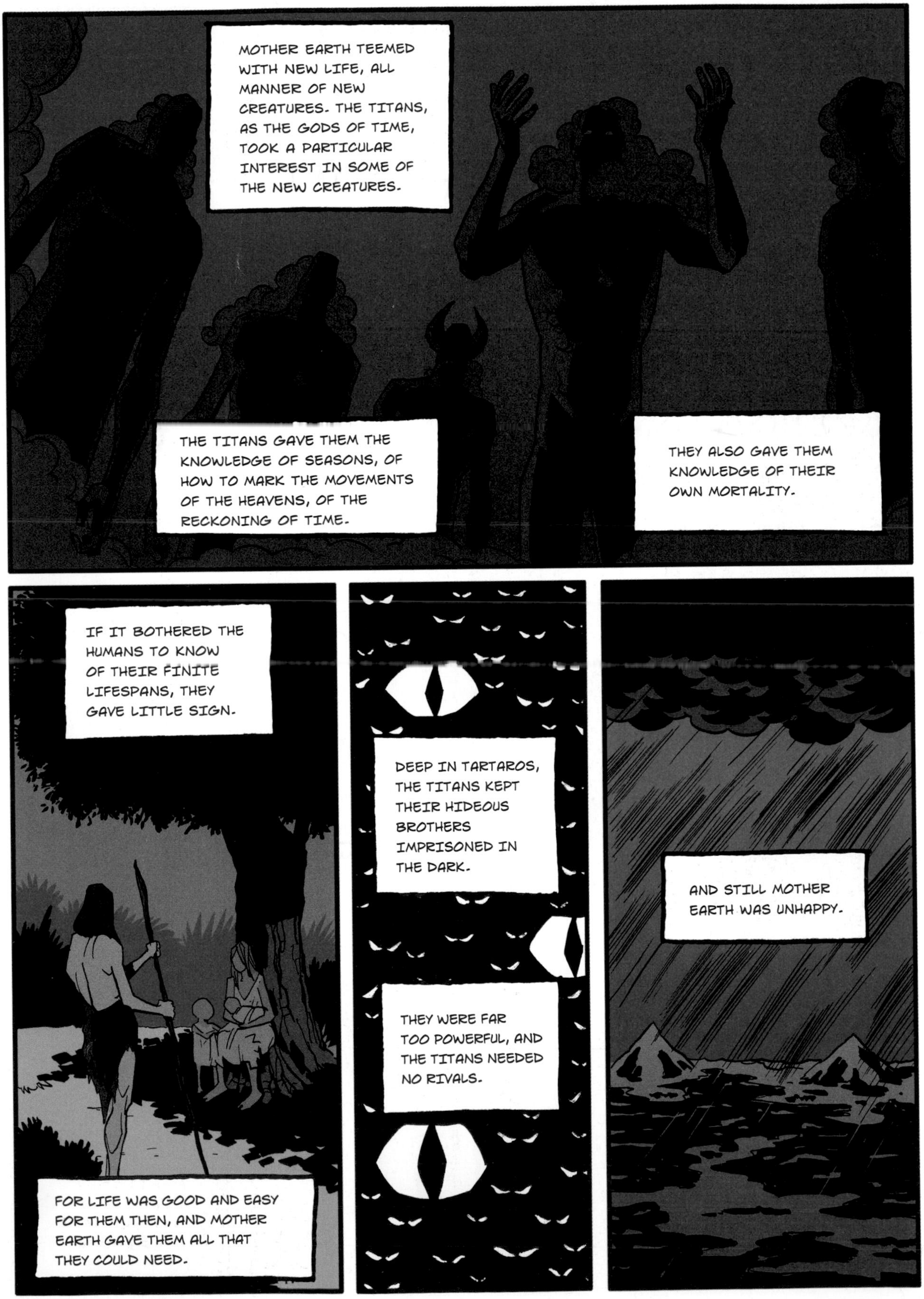

MOTHER EARTH TEEMED WITH NEW LIFE, ALL MANNER OF NEW CREATURES. THE TITANS, AS THE GODS OF TIME, TOOK A PARTICULAR INTEREST IN SOME OF THE NEW CREATURES.
THE TITANS GAVE THEM THE KNOWLEDGE OF SEASONS, OF HOW TO MARK THE MOVEMENTS OF THE HEAVENS, OF THE RECKONING OF TIME.
THEY ALSO GAVE THEM KNOWLEDGE OF THEIR OWN MORTALITY.
IF IT BOTHERED THE HUMANS TO KNOW OF THEIR FINITE LIFESPANS, THEY GAVE LITTLE SIGN.
FOR LIFE WAS GOOD AND EASY FOR THEM THEN, AND MOTHER EARTH GAVE THEM ALL THAT THEY COULD NEED.
DEEP IN TARTAROS, THE TITANS KEPT THEIR HIDEOUS BROTHERS IMPRISONED IN THE DARK.
THEY WERE FAR TOO POWERFUL, AND THE TITANS NEEDED NO RIVALS.
AND STILL MOTHER EARTH WAS UNHAPPY.

KRONOS WAS NOW THE LORD OF THE UNIVERSE.

HE TOOK HIS SISTER, THE TITANESS RHEA, AS HIS QUEEN AND HE RULED FROM ON HIGH.

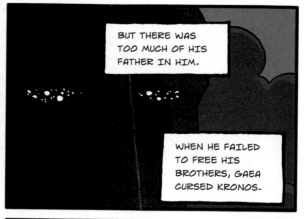

BUT THERE WAS TOO MUCH OF HIS FATHER IN HIM.

WHEN HE FAILED TO FREE HIS BROTHERS, GAEA CURSED KRONOS.

AS YOU HAVE OVERTHROWN YOUR FATHER, SO SHALL YOUR CHILD OVERTHROW YOU!

KRONOS HAD NO DESIRE TO SURRENDER HIS THRONE.

IN TIME, WHEN RHEA GAVE BIRTH TO THEIR DAUGHTER,

KRONOS, LORD OF THE UNIVERSE, REACHED DOWN, TOOK HIS FIRST-BORN CHILD IN HIS ARMS...

AND SWALLOWED HER WHOLE.

HE DID THIS WITH EACH OF HIS FIVE CHILDREN.

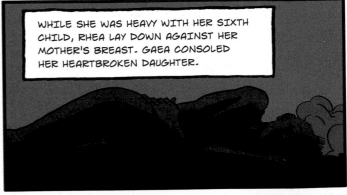

WHILE SHE WAS HEAVY WITH HER SIXTH CHILD, RHEA LAY DOWN AGAINST HER MOTHER'S BREAST. GAEA CONSOLED HER HEARTBROKEN DAUGHTER.

CAN YOU HEAR ME, MY DAUGHTER?

I, TOO, KNOW THE PAIN YOU FEEL. I TOO HAVE HAD MY CHILDREN LOCKED AWAY IN THE DARK.

CRAFTY KRONOS MAY THINK THAT HE HAS WON, BUT EVEN HE CANNOT ESCAPE FATE...

WHEN RHEA GAVE BIRTH TO HER SIXTH CHILD, A SWITCH WAS MADE. A CRUDE STONE LIKENESS WAS FORMED, AND WRAPPED IN SWADDLING CLOTHES.

IF LORD KRONOS NOTICED HIS NEWBORN SON HAD LESS WARMTH THAN THE REST, HE GAVE NO SIGN.

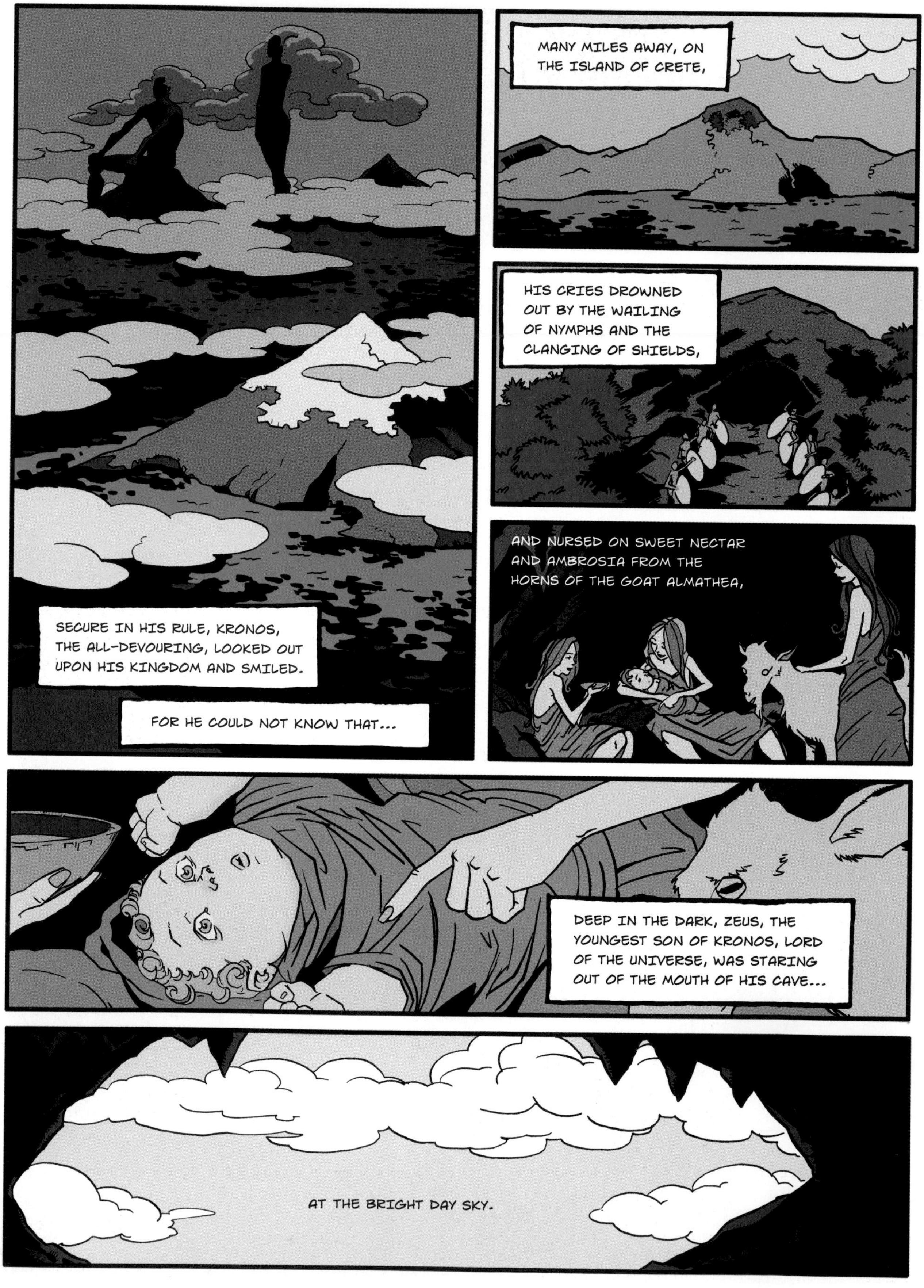
SECURE IN HIS RULE, KRONOS, THE ALL-DEVOURING, LOOKED OUT UPON HIS KINGDOM AND SMILED.
FOR HE COULD NOT KNOW THAT...
MANY MILES AWAY, ON THE ISLAND OF CRETE,
HIS CRIES DROWNED OUT BY THE WAILING OF NYMPHS AND THE CLANGING OF SHIELDS,
AND NURSED ON SWEET NECTAR AND AMBROSIA FROM THE HORNS OF THE GOAT ALMATHEA,
DEEP IN THE DARK, ZEUS, THE YOUNGEST SON OF KRONOS, LORD OF THE UNIVERSE, WAS STARING OUT OF THE MOUTH OF HIS CAVE...
AT THE BRIGHT DAY SKY.

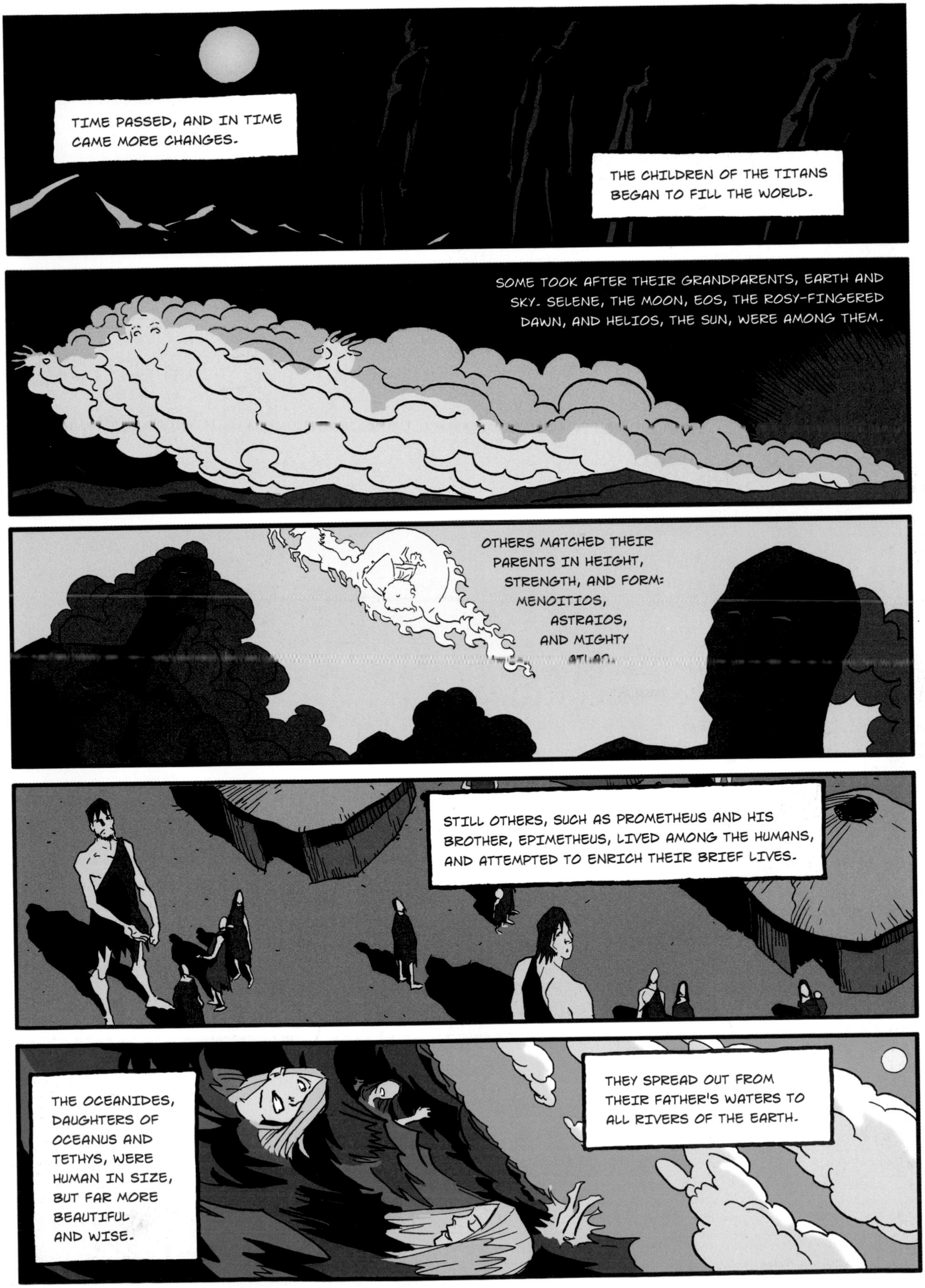
TIME PASSED, AND IN TIME CAME MORE CHANGES.
THE CHILDREN OF THE TITANS BEGAN TO FILL THE WORLD.
SOME TOOK AFTER THEIR GRANDPARENTS, EARTH AND SKY. SELENE, THE MOON, EOS, THE ROSY-FINGERED DAWN, AND HELIOS, THE SUN, WERE AMONG THEM.
OTHERS MATCHED THEIR PARENTS IN HEIGHT, STRENGTH, AND FORM: MENOITIOS, ASTRAIOS, AND MIGHTY
STILL OTHERS, SUCH AS PROMETHEUS AND HIS BROTHER, EPIMETHEUS, LIVED AMONG THE HUMANS, AND ATTEMPTED TO ENRICH THEIR BRIEF LIVES.
THE OCEANIDES, DAUGHTERS OF OCEANUS AND TETHYS, WERE HUMAN IN SIZE, BUT FAR MORE BEAUTIFUL AND WISE.
THEY SPREAD OUT FROM THEIR FATHER'S WATERS TO ALL RIVERS OF THE EARTH.

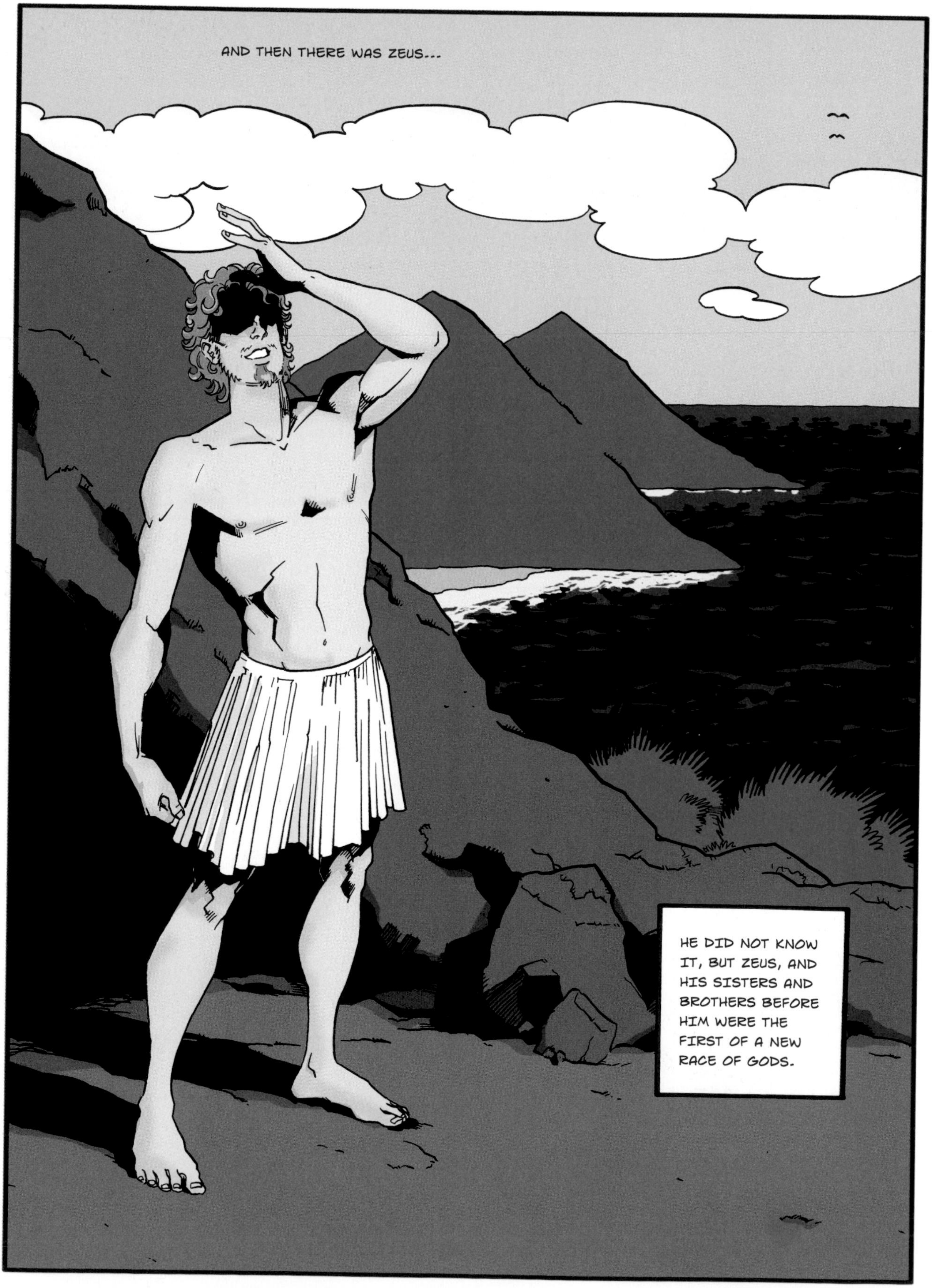
AND THEN THERE WAS ZEUS...
HE DID NOT KNOW IT, BUT ZEUS, AND HIS SISTERS AND BROTHERS BEFORE HIM WERE THE FIRST OF A NEW RACE OF GODS.

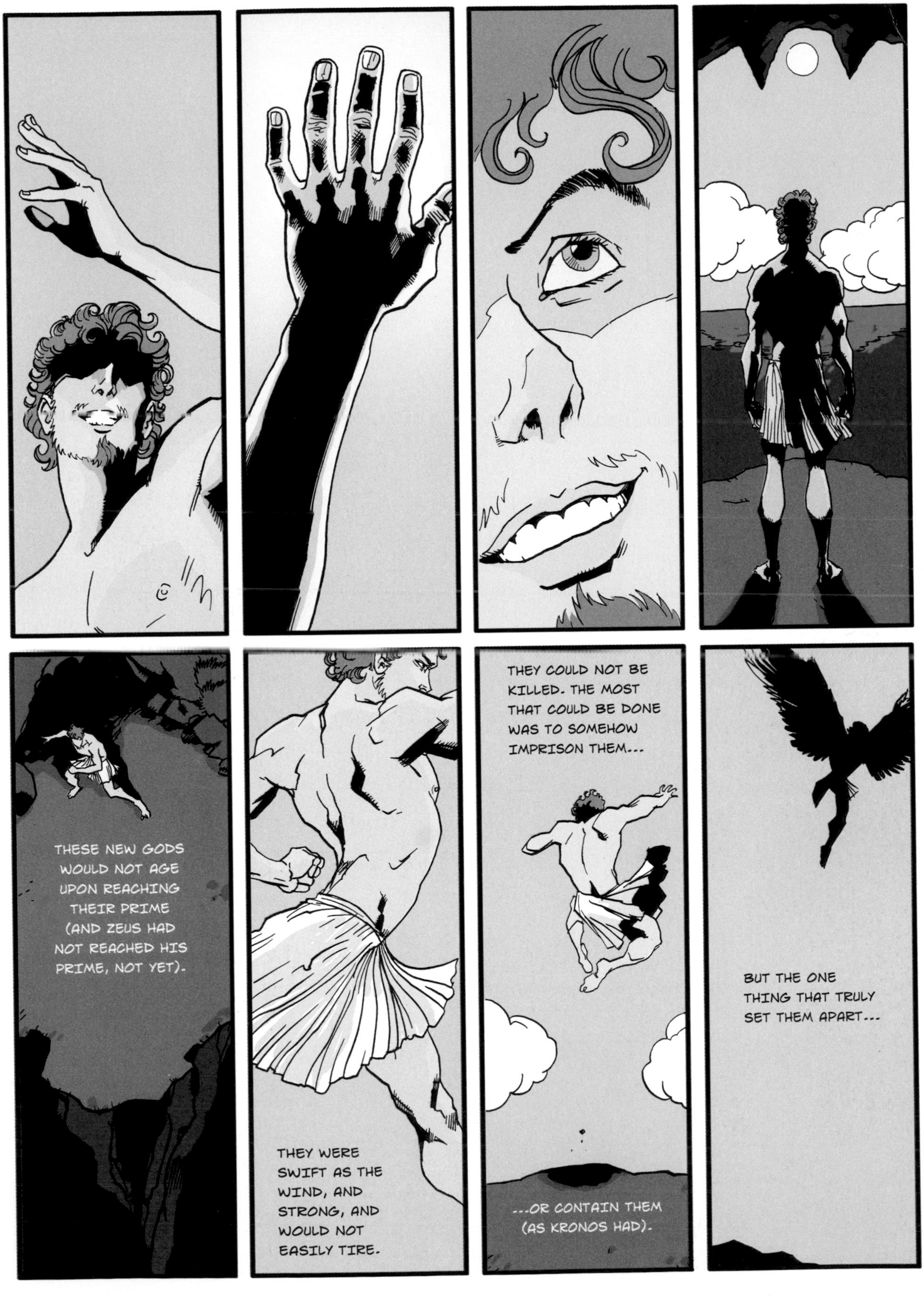
THESE NEW GODS WOULD NOT AGE UPON REACHING THEIR PRIME (AND ZEUS HAD NOT REACHED HIS PRIME, NOT YET).
THEY WERE SWIFT AS THE WIND, AND STRONG, AND WOULD NOT EASILY TIRE.
THEY COULD NOT BE KILLED. THE MOST THAT COULD BE DONE WAS TO SOMEHOW IMPRISON THEM...
...OR CONTAIN THEM (AS KRONOS HAD).
BUT THE ONE THING THAT TRULY SET THEM APART...

...WAS THEIR ABILITY TO TRANSFORM.

TO BE AN OLYMPIAN (AS THESE NEW GODS WOULD COME TO BE CALLED) WAS TO BE ABLE TO CHANGE SHAPE AS OTHERS CHANGE THEIR MIND.

INTO ANYTHING THEY DESIRED...

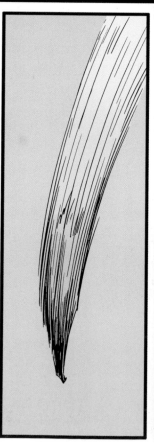

SHAPES FLOWING INTO SHAPES...

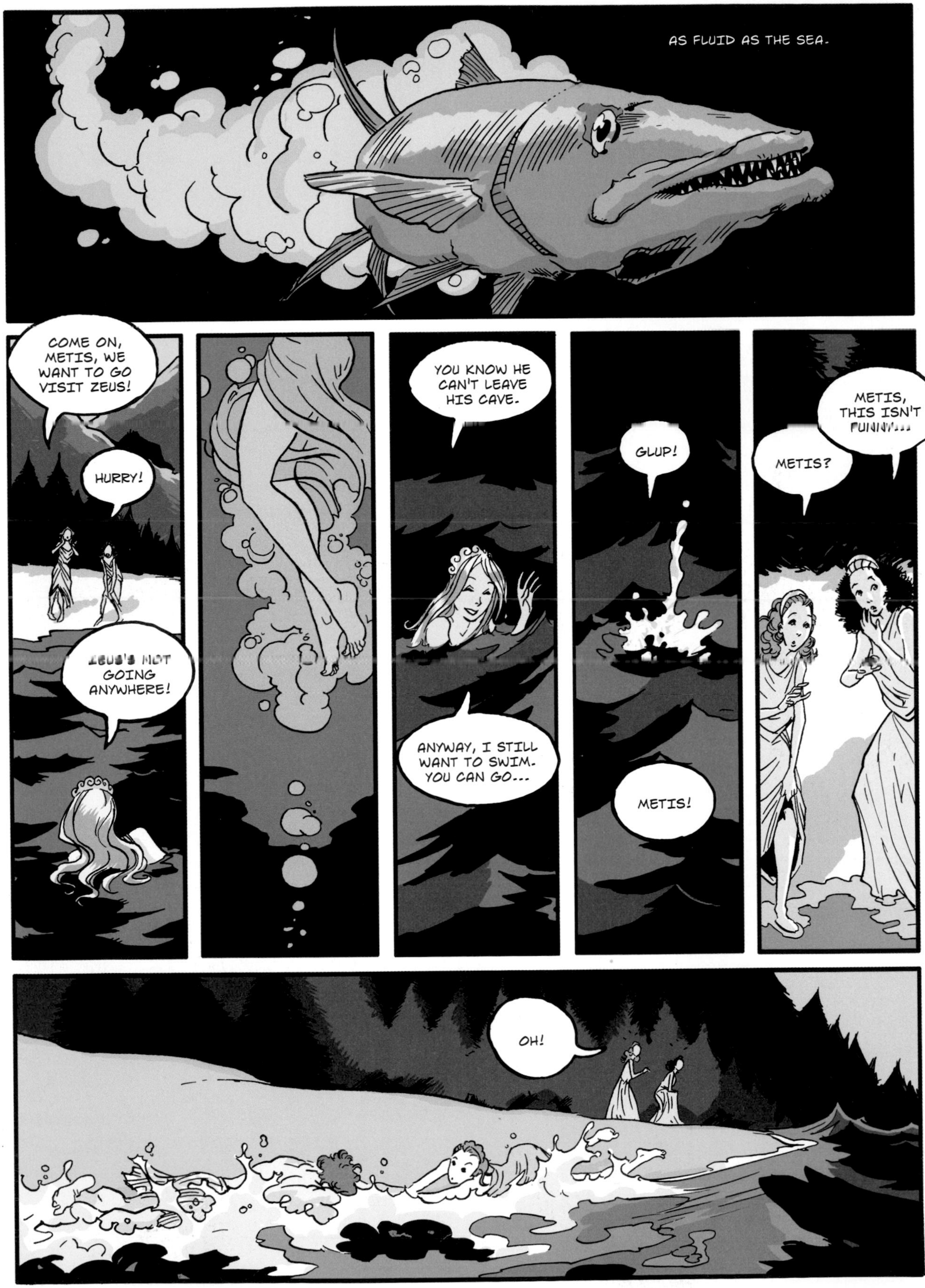
AS FLUID AS THE SEA.
COME ON, METIS, WE WANT TO GO VISIT ZEUS!
HURRY!
ZEUS'S NOT GOING ANYWHERE!
YOU KNOW HE CAN'T LEAVE HIS CAVE.
ANYWAY, I STILL WANT TO SWIM. YOU CAN GO...
GLUP!
METIS!
METIS, THIS ISN'T FUNNY...
METIS?
OH!

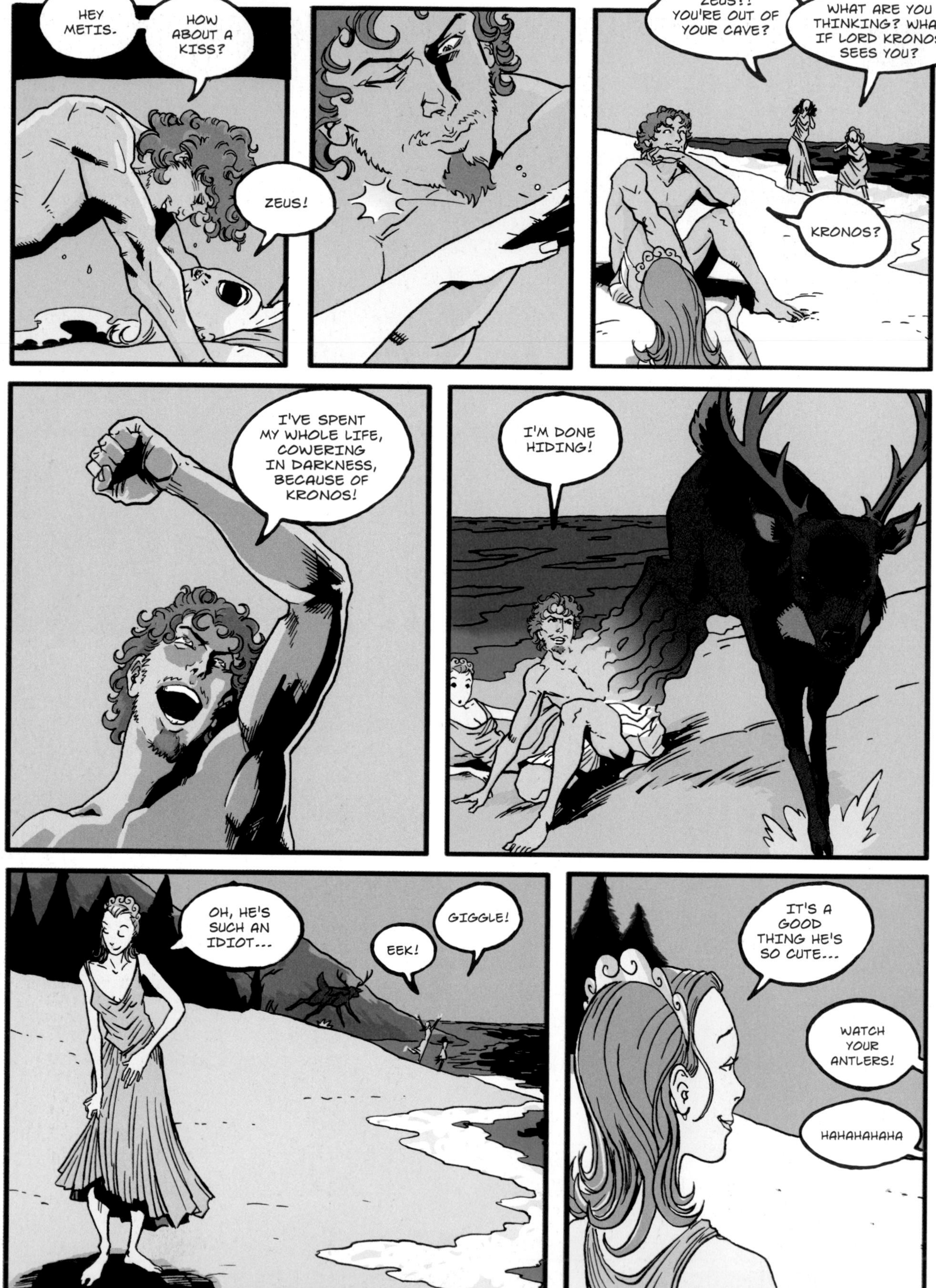
HEY METIS.
HOW ABOUT A KISS?
ZEUS!
ZEUS?! YOU'RE OUT OF YOUR CAVE?
WHAT ARE YOU THINKING? WHAT IF LORD KRONOS SEES YOU?
KRONOS?
I'VE SPENT MY WHOLE LIFE, COWERING IN DARKNESS, BECAUSE OF KRONOS!
I'M DONE HIDING!
OH, HE'S SUCH AN IDIOT...
EEK!
GIGGLE!
IT'S A GOOD THING HE'S SO CUTE...
WATCH YOUR ANTLERS!
HAHAHAHAHA

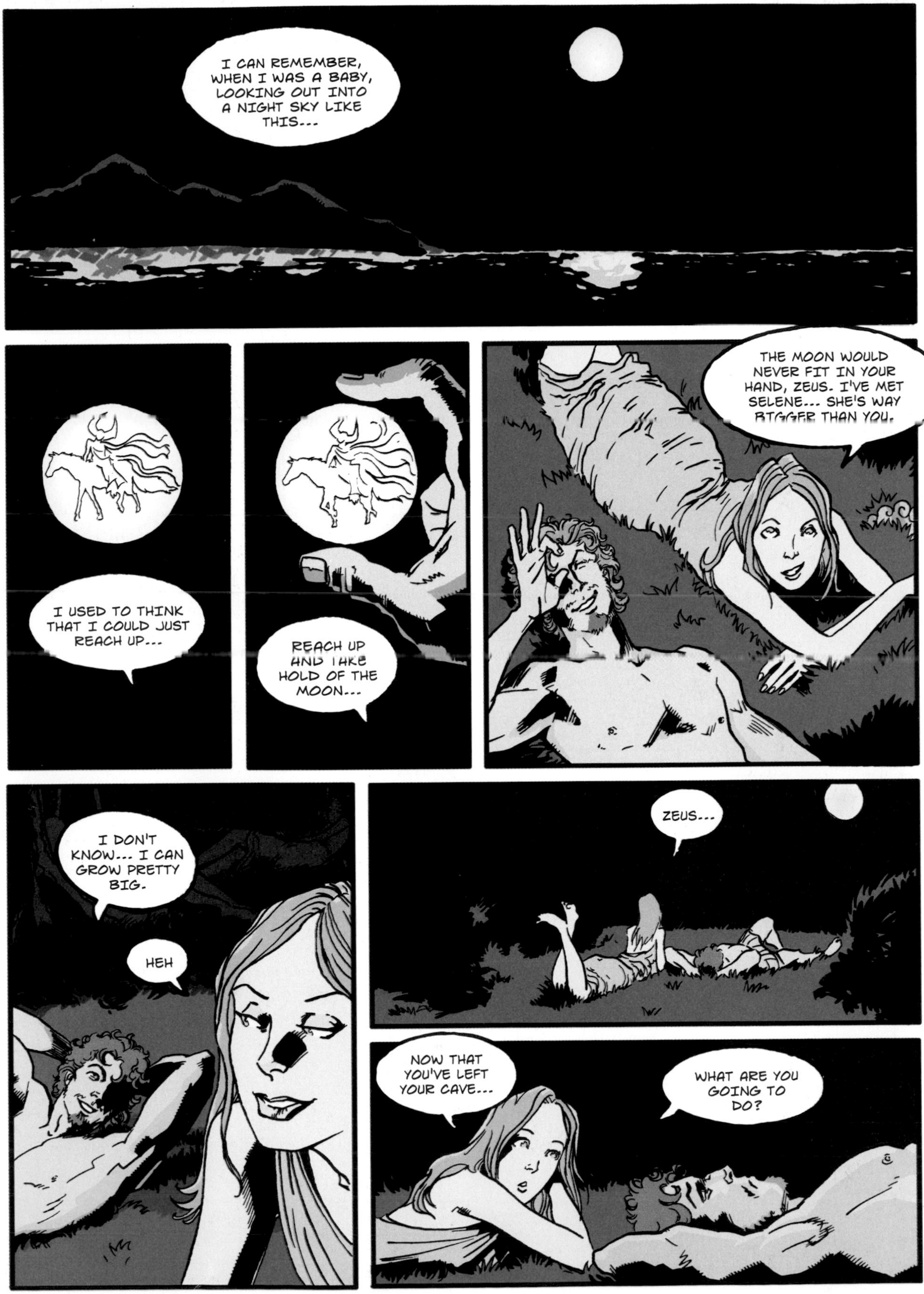
I CAN REMEMBER, WHEN I WAS A BABY, LOOKING OUT INTO A NIGHT SKY LIKE THIS...
I USED TO THINK THAT I COULD JUST REACH UP...
REACH UP AND TAKE HOLD OF THE MOON...
THE MOON WOULD NEVER FIT IN YOUR HAND, ZEUS. I'VE MET SELENE... SHE'S WAY BIGGER THAN YOU.
I DON'T KNOW... I CAN GROW PRETTY BIG.
HEH
ZEUS...
NOW THAT YOU'VE LEFT YOUR CAVE...
WHAT ARE YOU GOING TO DO?

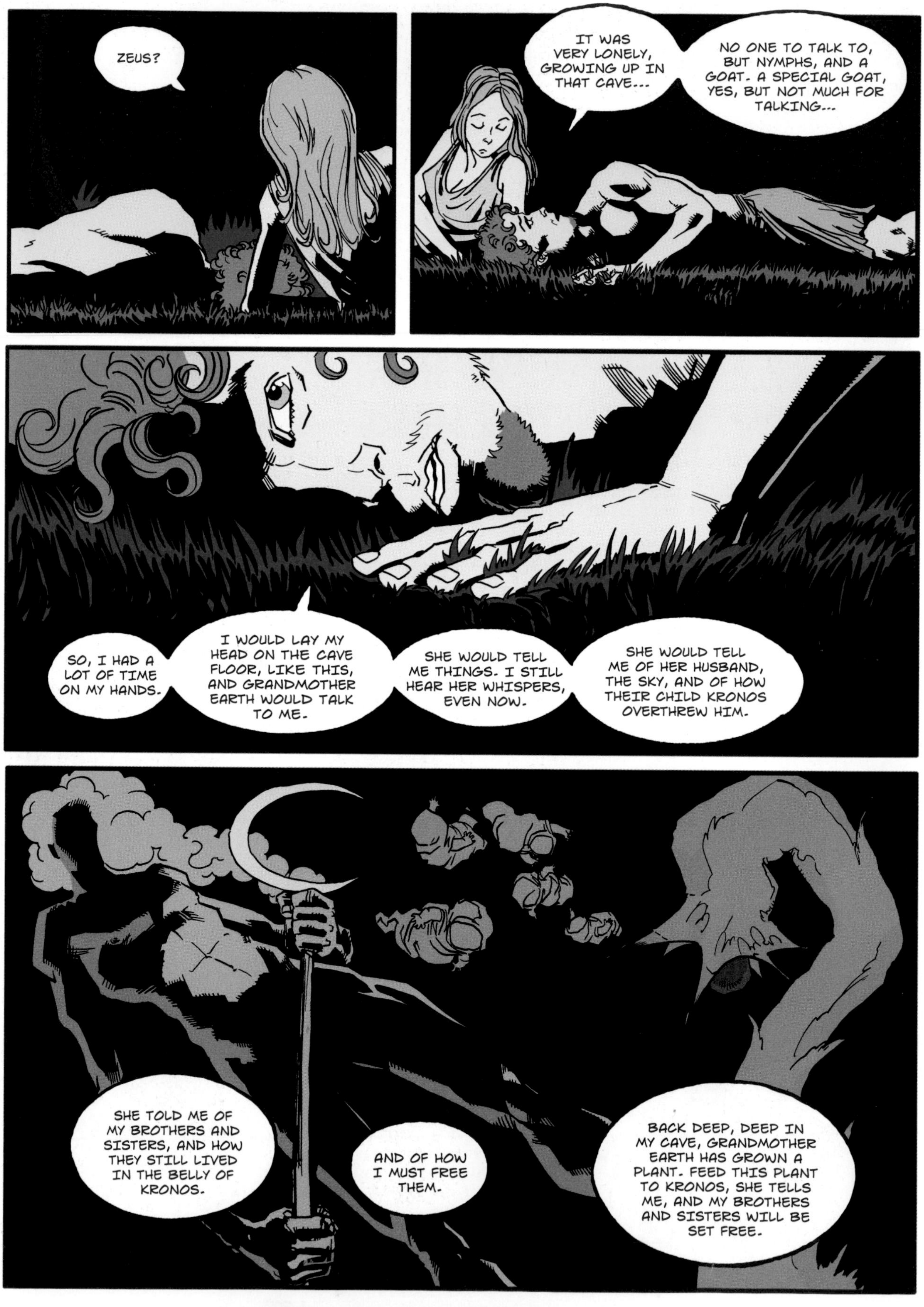

ZEUS?
IT WAS VERY LONELY, GROWING UP IN THAT CAVE...
NO ONE TO TALK TO, BUT NYMPHS, AND A GOAT. A SPECIAL GOAT, YES, BUT NOT MUCH FOR TALKING...
SO, I HAD A LOT OF TIME ON MY HANDS.
I WOULD LAY MY HEAD ON THE CAVE FLOOR, LIKE THIS, AND GRANDMOTHER EARTH WOULD TALK TO ME.
SHE WOULD TELL ME THINGS. I STILL HEAR HER WHISPERS, EVEN NOW.
SHE WOULD TELL ME OF HER HUSBAND, THE SKY, AND OF HOW THEIR CHILD KRONOS OVERTHREW HIM.
SHE TOLD ME OF MY BROTHERS AND SISTERS, AND HOW THEY STILL LIVED IN THE BELLY OF KRONOS.
AND OF HOW I MUST FREE THEM.
BACK DEEP, DEEP IN MY CAVE, GRANDMOTHER EARTH HAS GROWN A PLANT. FEED THIS PLANT TO KRONOS, SHE TELLS ME, AND MY BROTHERS AND SISTERS WILL BE SET FREE.

OF COURSE, SHE HASN'T TOLD ME EXACTLY HOW I'M SUPPOSED TO GET THIS PLANT TO KRONOS.

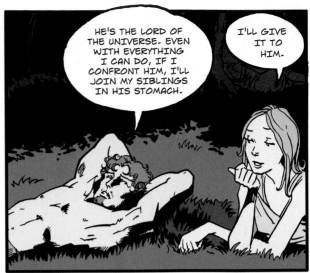

HE'S THE LORD OF THE UNIVERSE. EVEN WITH EVERYTHING I CAN DO, IF I CONFRONT HIM, I'LL JOIN MY SIBLINGS IN HIS STOMACH.

I'LL GIVE IT TO HIM.

WHAT?

KRONOS IS MY UNCLE. AS FAR AS HE KNOWS, HE'S GOT NOTHING TO FEAR FROM ME.

I'LL FEED HIM THE PLANT AND HE'LL COUGH UP YOUR BROTHERS AND SISTERS. THEN YOU ALL GET TOGETHER, OVERTHROW THE TITANS, AND BOOM! YOU'RE THE NEW LORD OF THE UNIVERSE.

YOU MAKE IT SOUND SO EASY.

ISN'T IT? YOU HAVE ME HELPING YOU, AFTER ALL.

HA!

AND THEN, WHEN YOU'RE THE NEW LORD OF THE UNIVERSE, YOU'LL MAKE ME YOUR QUEEN.

I WILL, HUH? HOW COME?

BECAUSE I'M SO MUCH SMARTER THAN YOU, OF COURSE.

OF COURSE!

LISTEN TO ME, ZEUS: YOU'LL GO FAR. HERE'S THE PLAN.

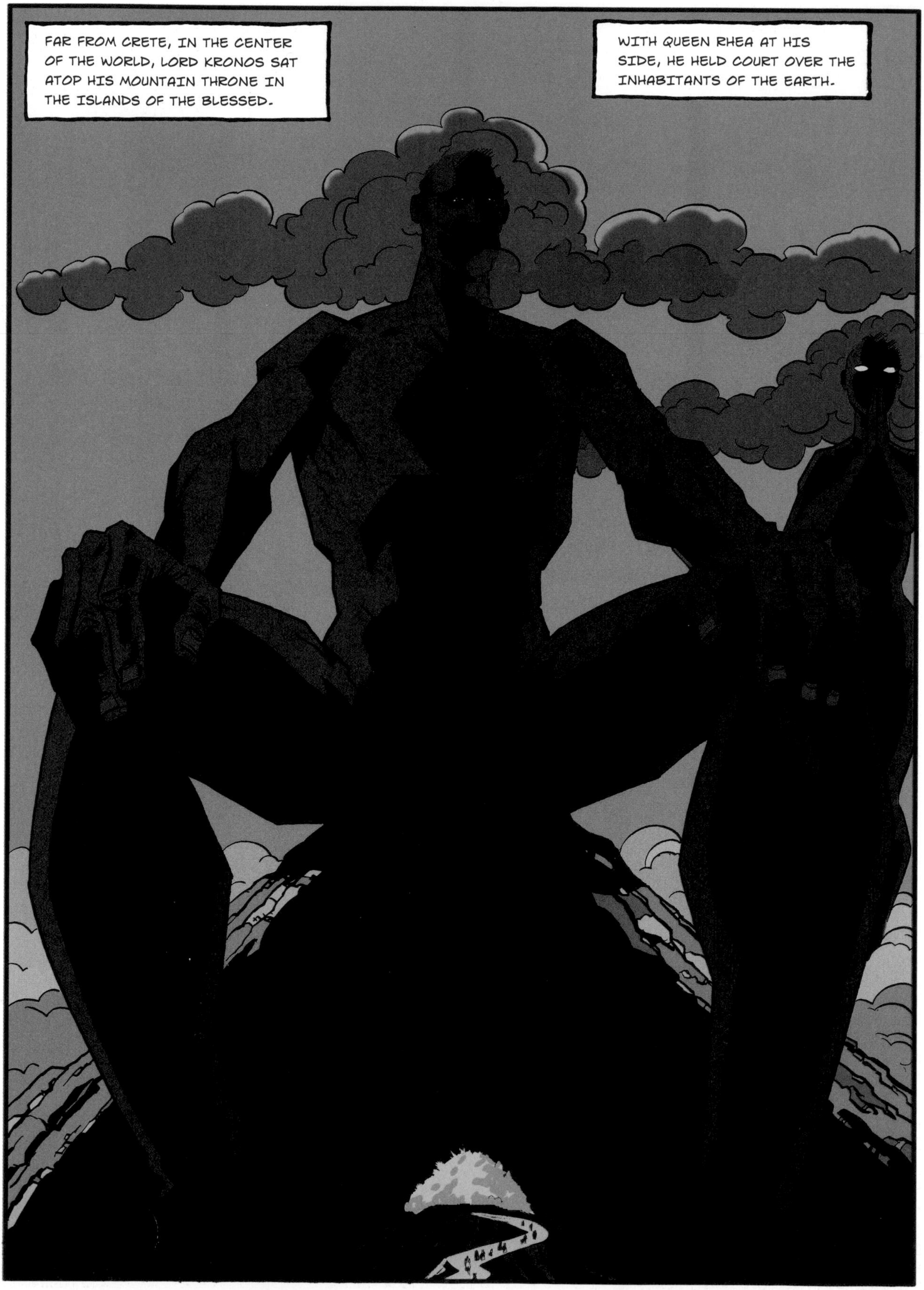
FAR FROM CRETE, IN THE CENTER OF THE WORLD, LORD KRONOS SAT ATOP HIS MOUNTAIN THRONE IN THE ISLANDS OF THE BLESSED.
WITH QUEEN RHEA AT HIS SIDE, HE HELD COURT OVER THE INHABITANTS OF THE EARTH.

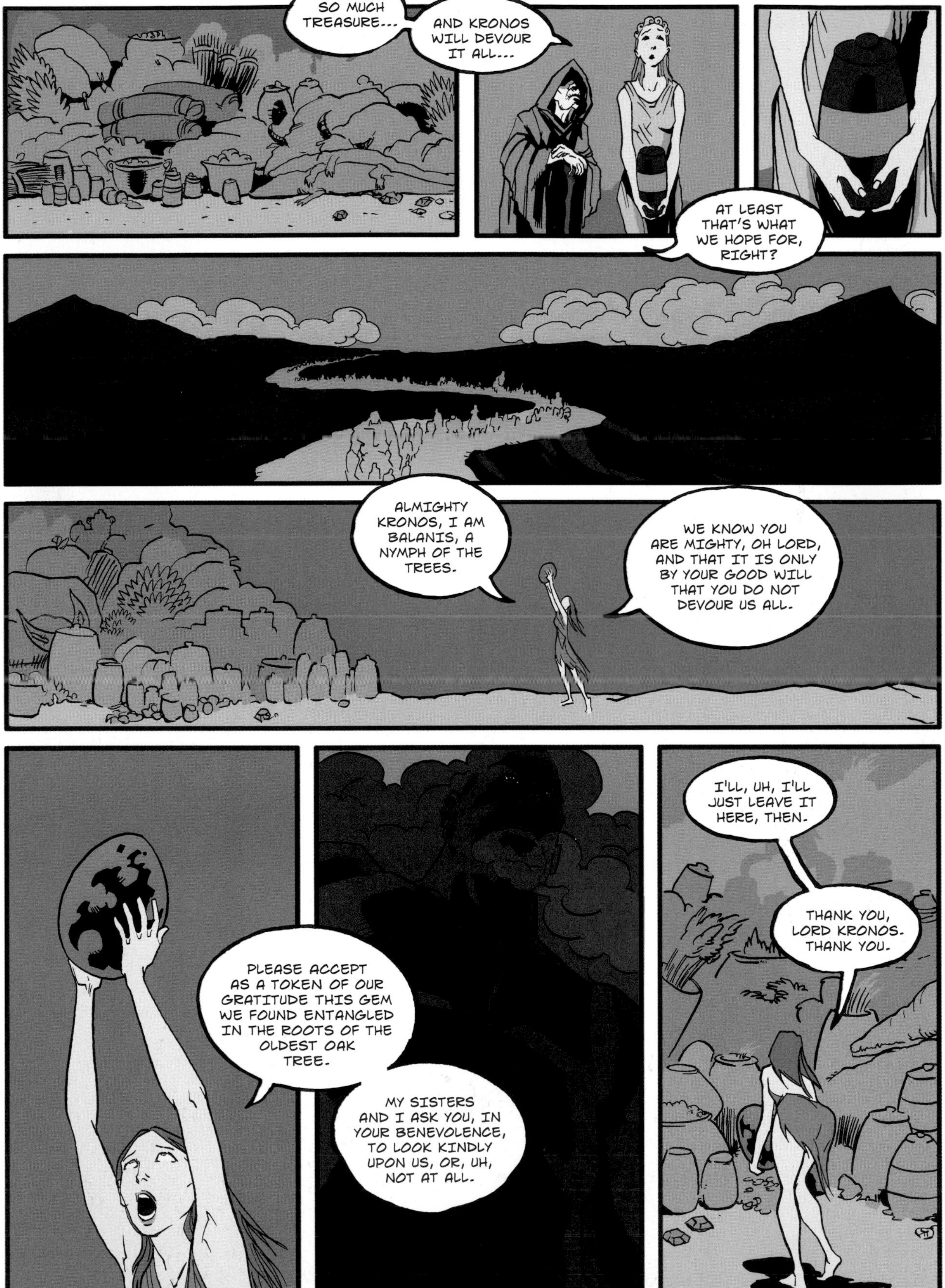
SO MUCH TREASURE...
AND KRONOS WILL DEVOUR IT ALL...
AT LEAST THAT'S WHAT WE HOPE FOR, RIGHT?
ALMIGHTY KRONOS, I AM BALANIS, A NYMPH OF THE TREES.
WE KNOW YOU ARE MIGHTY, OH LORD, AND THAT IT IS ONLY BY YOUR GOOD WILL THAT YOU DO NOT DEVOUR US ALL.
PLEASE ACCEPT AS A TOKEN OF OUR GRATITUDE THIS GEM WE FOUND ENTANGLED IN THE ROOTS OF THE OLDEST OAK TREE.
MY SISTERS AND I ASK YOU, IN YOUR BENEVOLENCE, TO LOOK KINDLY UPON US, OR, UH, NOT AT ALL.
I'LL, UH, I'LL JUST LEAVE IT HERE, THEN.
THANK YOU, LORD KRONOS. THANK YOU.

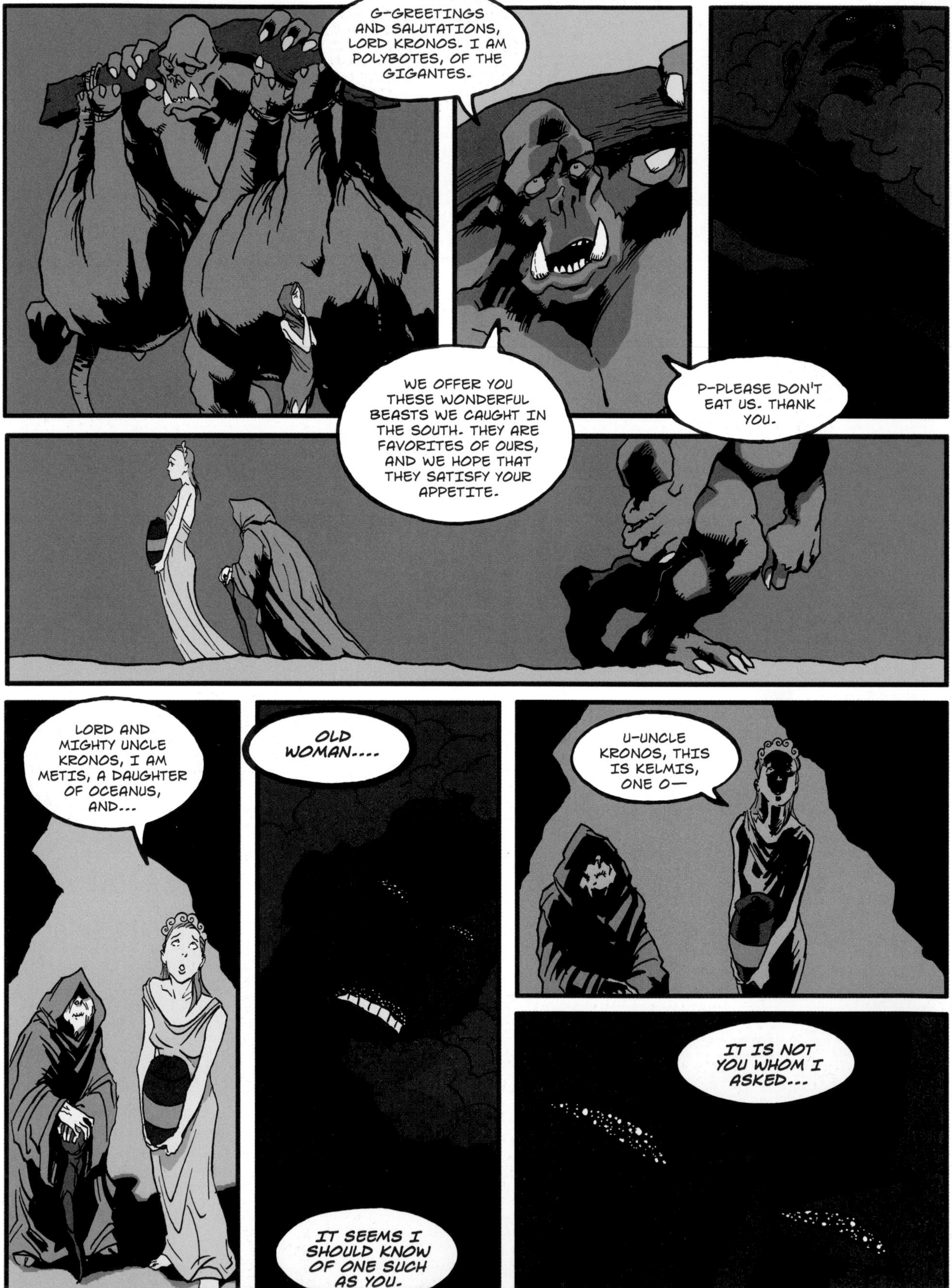

G-GREETINGS AND SALUTATIONS, LORD KRONOS. I AM POLYBOTES, OF THE GIGANTES.
WE OFFER YOU THESE WONDERFUL BEASTS WE CAUGHT IN THE SOUTH. THEY ARE FAVORITES OF OURS, AND WE HOPE THAT THEY SATISFY YOUR APPETITE.
P-PLEASE DON'T EAT US. THANK YOU.
LORD AND MIGHTY UNCLE KRONOS, I AM METIS, A DAUGHTER OF OCEANUS, AND...
OLD WOMAN....
IT SEEMS I SHOULD KNOW OF ONE SUCH AS YOU.
U-UNCLE KRONOS, THIS IS KELMIS, ONE O—
IT IS NOT YOU WHOM I ASKED...

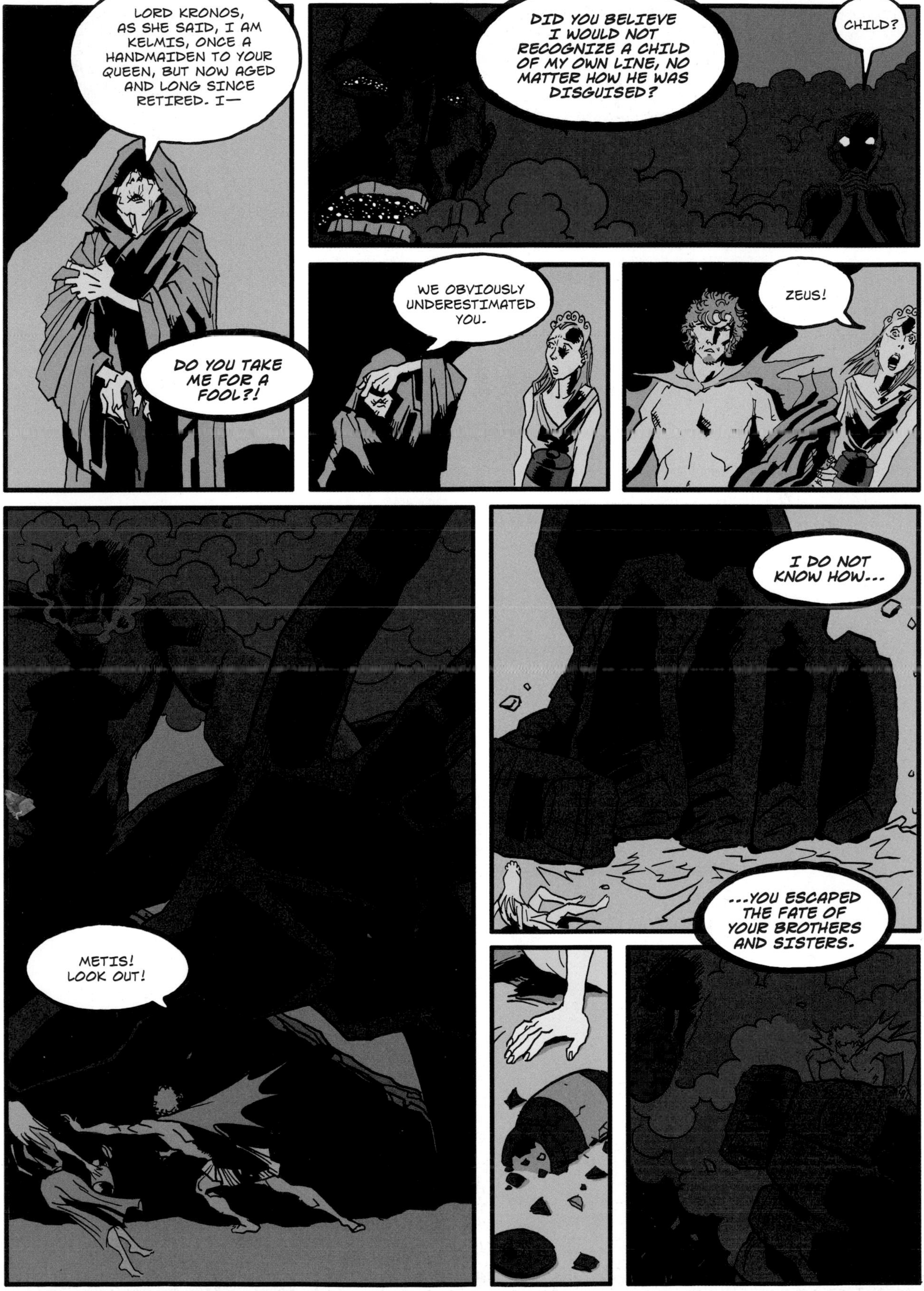
LORD KRONOS, AS SHE SAID, I AM KELMIS, ONCE A HANDMAIDEN TO YOUR QUEEN, BUT NOW AGED AND LONG SINCE RETIRED. I—
DO YOU TAKE ME FOR A FOOL?!
DID YOU BELIEVE I WOULD NOT RECOGNIZE A CHILD OF MY OWN LINE, NO MATTER HOW HE WAS DISGUISED?
CHILD?
WE OBVIOUSLY UNDERESTIMATED YOU.
ZEUS!
METIS! LOOK OUT!
I DO NOT KNOW HOW...
...YOU ESCAPED THE FATE OF YOUR BROTHERS AND SISTERS.

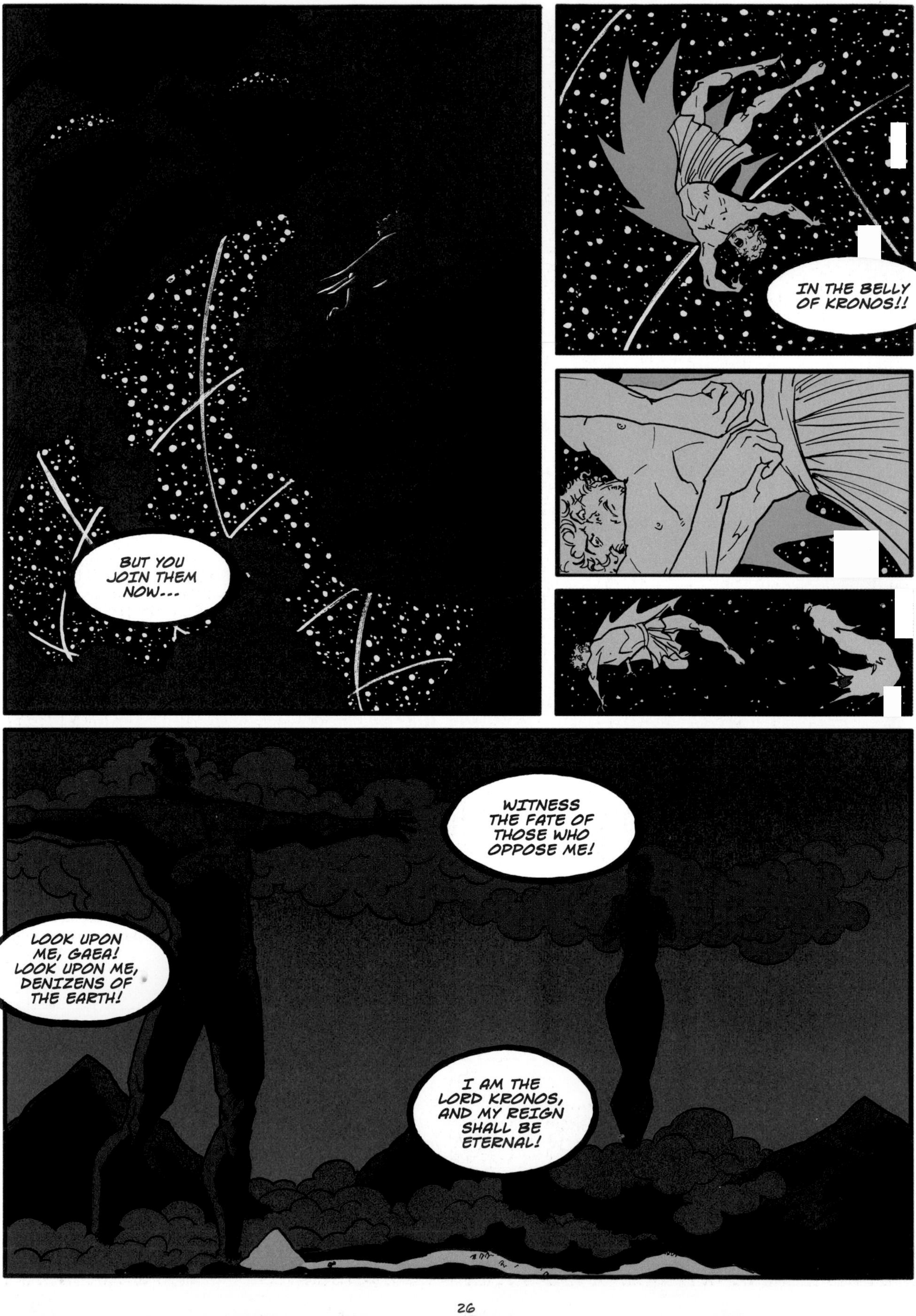
BUT YOU JOIN THEM NOW...
IN THE BELLY OF KRONOS!!
WITNESS THE FATE OF THOSE WHO OPPOSE ME!
LOOK UPON ME, GAEA! LOOK UPON ME, DENIZENS OF THE EARTH!
I AM THE LORD KRONOS, AND MY REIGN SHALL BE ETERNAL!

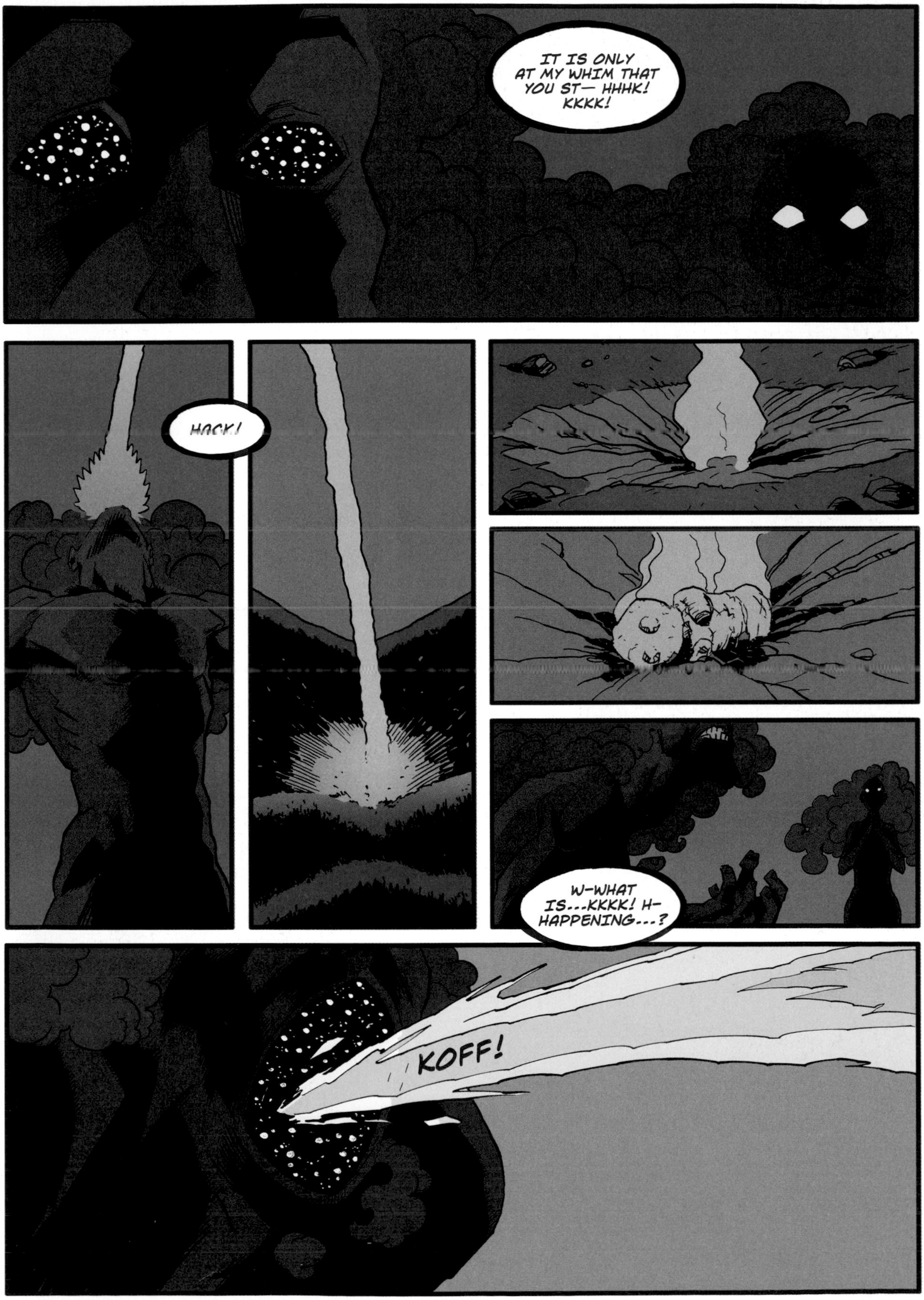
IT IS ONLY AT MY WHIM THAT YOU ST— HHHK! KKKK!
HACK!
W-WHAT IS...KKKK! H-HAPPENING...?
KOFF!

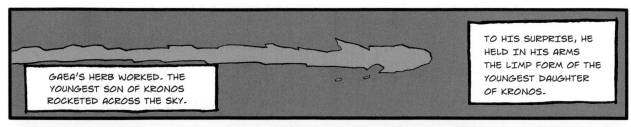

GAEA'S HERB WORKED. THE YOUNGEST SON OF KRONOS ROCKETED ACROSS THE SKY.

TO HIS SURPRISE, HE HELD IN HIS ARMS THE LIMP FORM OF THE YOUNGEST DAUGHTER OF KRONOS.

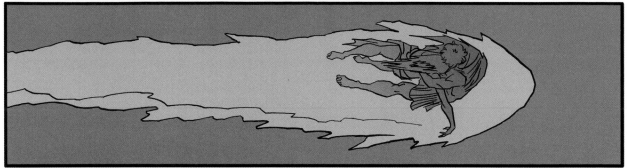

GROWN TO ADULTHOOD IN KRONOS'S BELLY, SHE WAS THE MOST BEAUTIFUL CREATURE HE HAD EVER SEEN.

HER NAME WAS HERA.

MMM...OH. HELLO.

H-HELLO. MY NAME IS ZEUS.

28

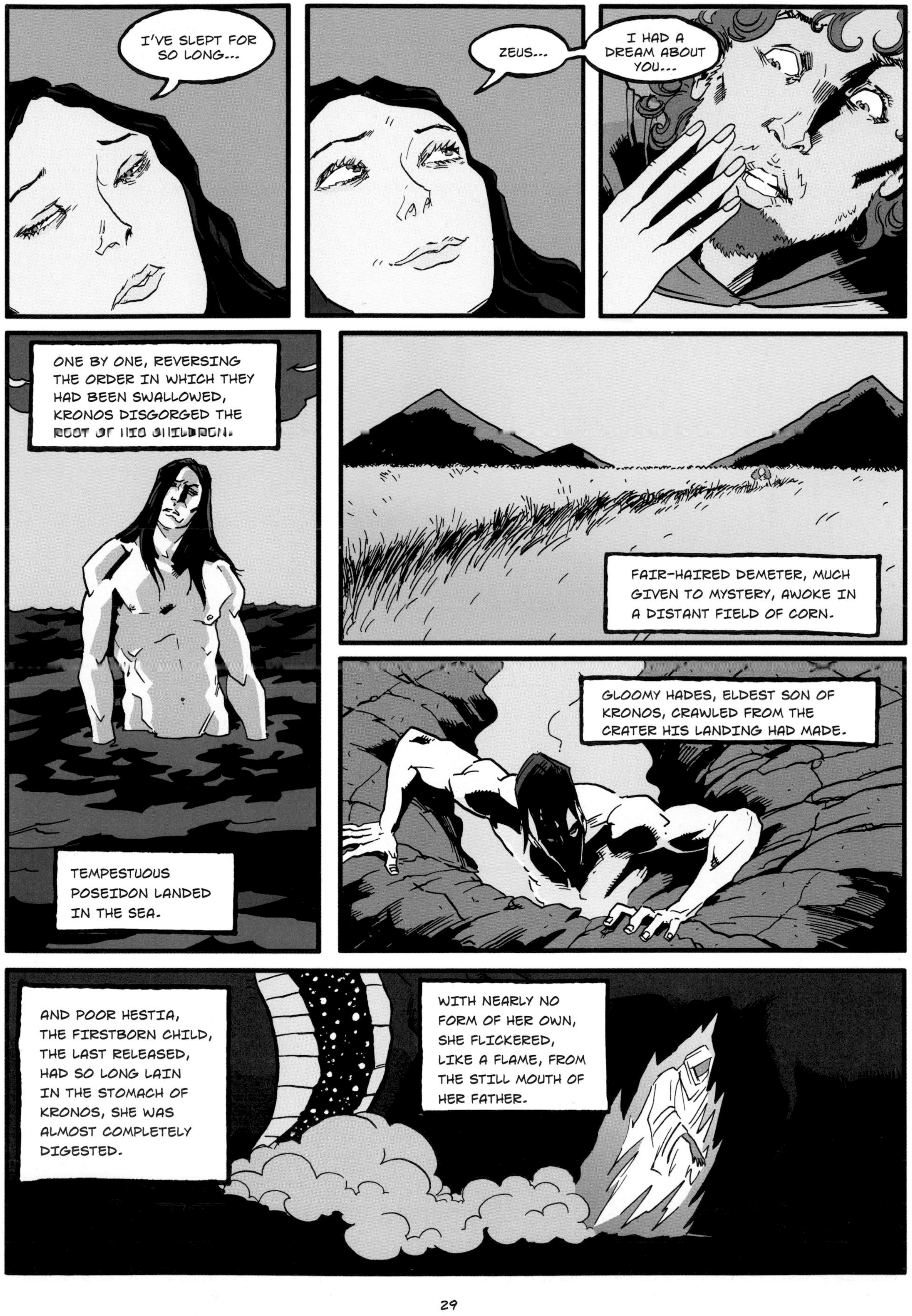
I'VE SLEPT FOR SO LONG...
ZEUS...
I HAD A DREAM ABOUT YOU...
ONE BY ONE, REVERSING THE ORDER IN WHICH THEY HAD BEEN SWALLOWED, KRONOS DISGORGED THE REST OF HIS CHILDREN.
TEMPESTUOUS POSEIDON LANDED IN THE SEA.
FAIR-HAIRED DEMETER, MUCH GIVEN TO MYSTERY, AWOKE IN A DISTANT FIELD OF CORN.
GLOOMY HADES, ELDEST SON OF KRONOS, CRAWLED FROM THE CRATER HIS LANDING HAD MADE.
AND POOR HESTIA, THE FIRSTBORN CHILD, THE LAST RELEASED, HAD SO LONG LAIN IN THE STOMACH OF KRONOS, SHE WAS ALMOST COMPLETELY DIGESTED.
WITH NEARLY NO FORM OF HER OWN, SHE FLICKERED, LIKE A FLAME, FROM THE STILL MOUTH OF HER FATHER.

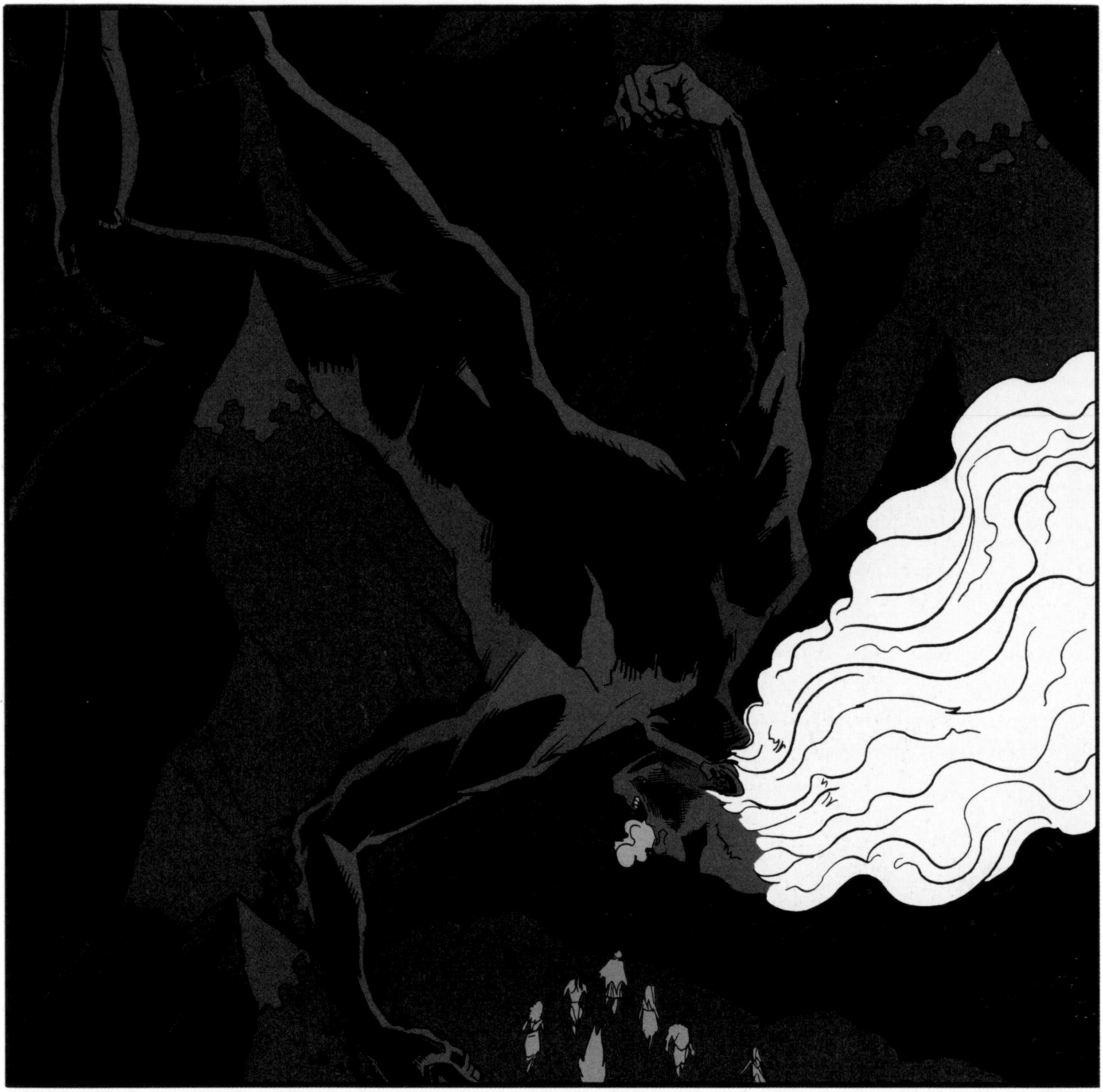

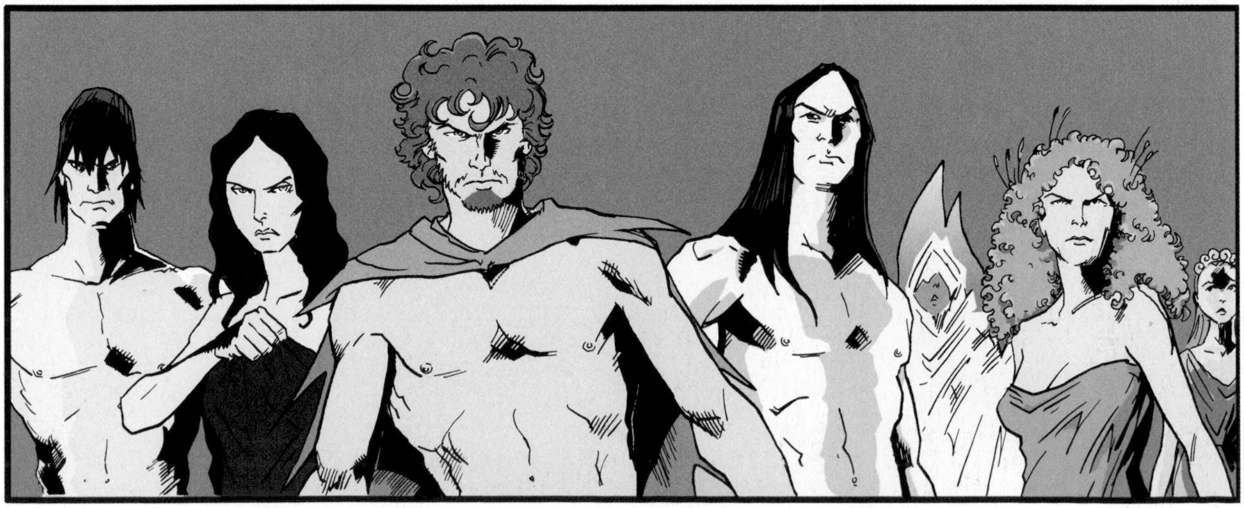

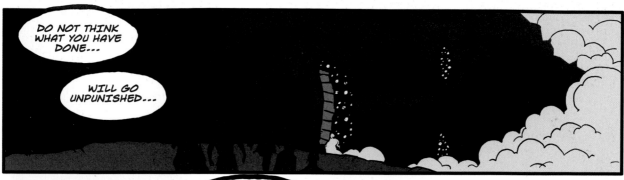

DO NOT THINK WHAT YOU HAVE DONE...

WILL GO UNPUNISHED...

ALREADY MY BROTHERS COME TO MY AID. ALREADY, MY STRENGTH RETURNS...

PROPHECY BE DAMNED. WE WILL.... I WILL...NOT BE BEATEN BY BRATS LIKE YOU...

IN TIME, WE WILL DESTROY YOU...

YOU HAVE HAD YOUR TIME IN THE SUN, FATHER.

ZEUS?

WE WILL TAKE WHAT WE DESERVE. WHAT WE HAVE BEEN DENIED FOR SO LONG.

ANY WHO STAND WITH KRONOS STAND AGAINST US.

GOODBYE.

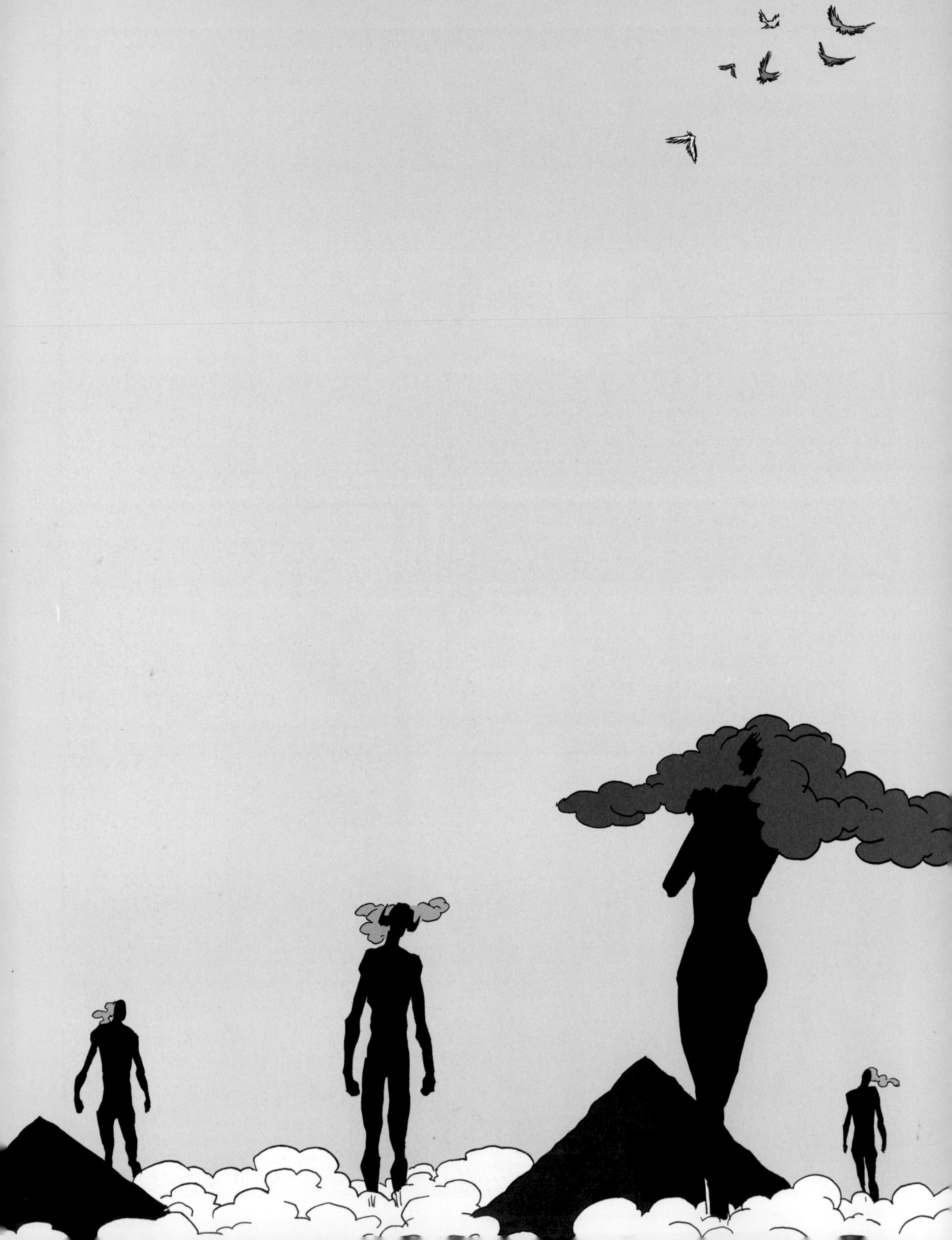

THE TITANESSES AND OCEANUS DID NOT JOIN IN THE CLASH. BUT THE TITANS...

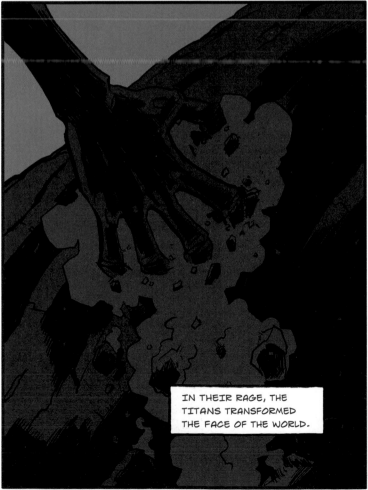

IN THEIR RAGE, THE TITANS TRANSFORMED THE FACE OF THE WORLD.

CONTINENTS WERE TORN FROM THE EARTH.

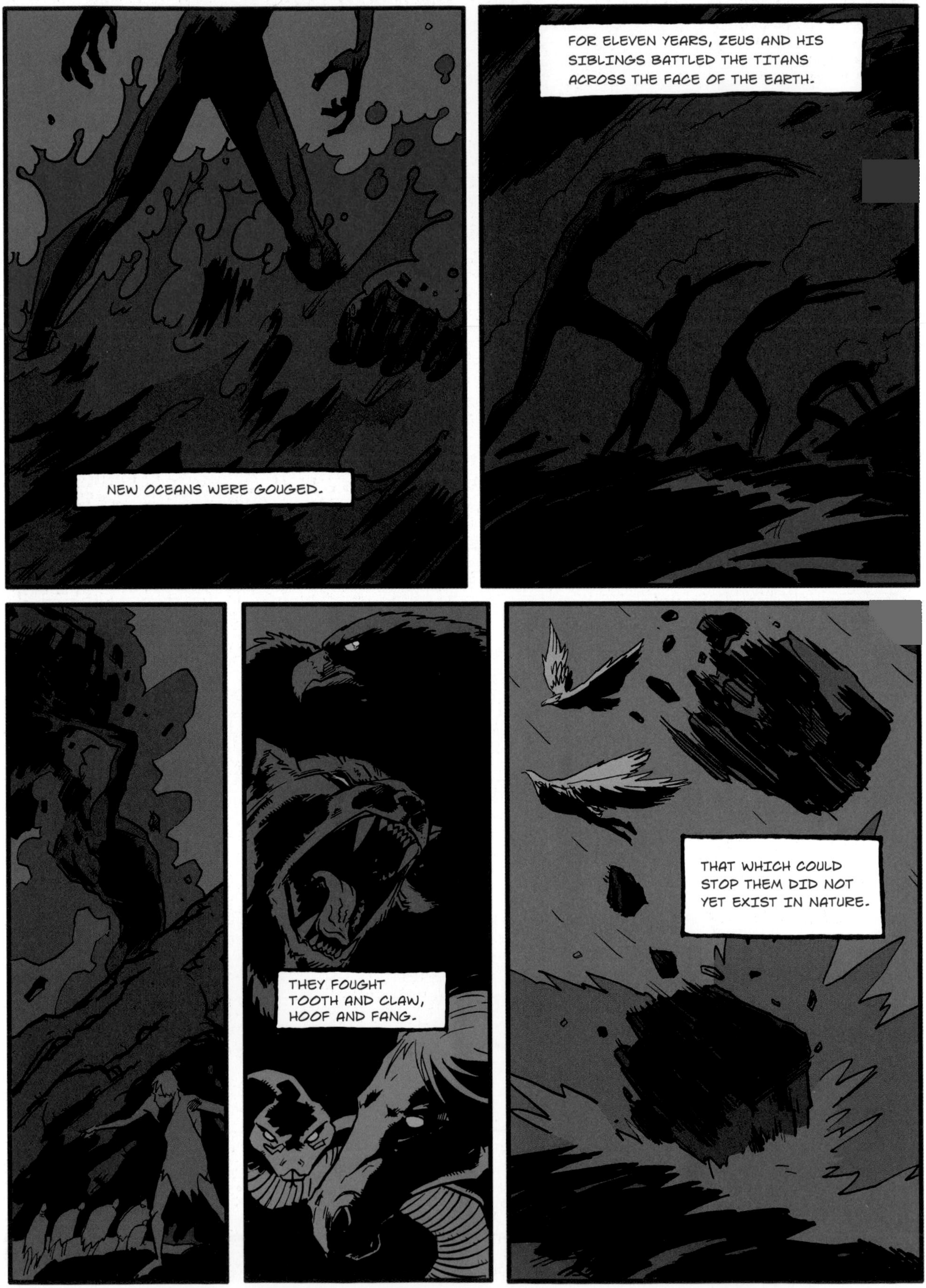
NEW OCEANS WERE GOUGED.
FOR ELEVEN YEARS, ZEUS AND HIS SIBLINGS BATTLED THE TITANS ACROSS THE FACE OF THE EARTH.
THEY FOUGHT TOOTH AND CLAW, HOOF AND FANG.
THAT WHICH COULD STOP THEM DID NOT YET EXIST IN NATURE.

EXHAUSTED, ZEUS TURNED TO GRANDMOTHER EARTH, AS HE HAD YEARS BEFORE.

LISTEN TO ME, MY BRAVE GRANDSON.

KNOW THIS: YOU MUST TRAVEL DEEP, DEEP WITHIN MY CRUST.

AS DEEP BELOW AS THE HEAVENS ABOVE ARE HIGH.

YOU MUST MAKE THIS JOURNEY ALONE.

IT WILL NOT BE WITHOUT DANGER.

TO MATCH THE TITANS' FURY, YOU MUST BREACH THE GATES OF TARTAROS.

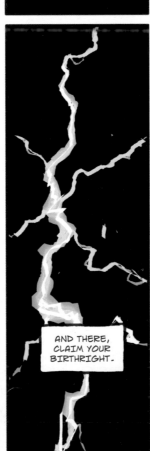

AND THERE, CLAIM YOUR BIRTHRIGHT.

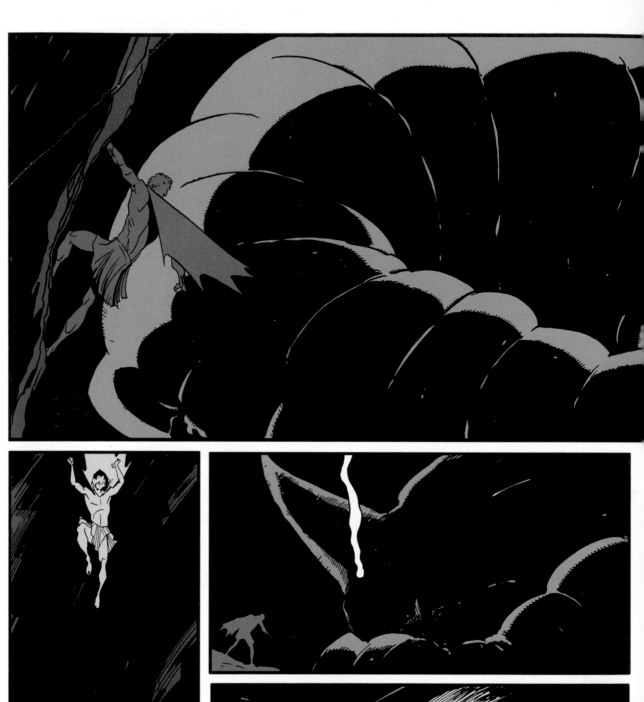

YOU WON'T GET PAST ME LIKE THAT, SON OF KRONOS.

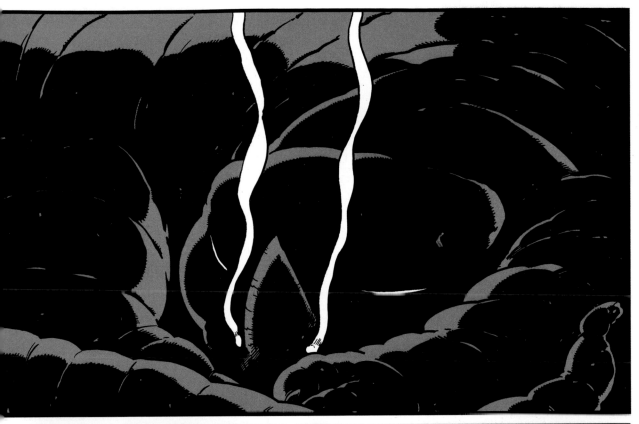

BUT I HAVE BEEN IN THIS CAVE SINCE THE TIME BEFORE TIME, AND HAVE GROWN VERY LARGE INDEED. THE GATEWAY TO TARTAROS IS VERY TIGHT, AND I FILL IT COMPLETELY

TRUST ME, O SON OF KRONOS, IN HERE, YOU CANNOT GROW LARGE ENOUGH TO CONTEND WITH ME.

I KNOW THAT YOU CAN GROW VERY LARGE.

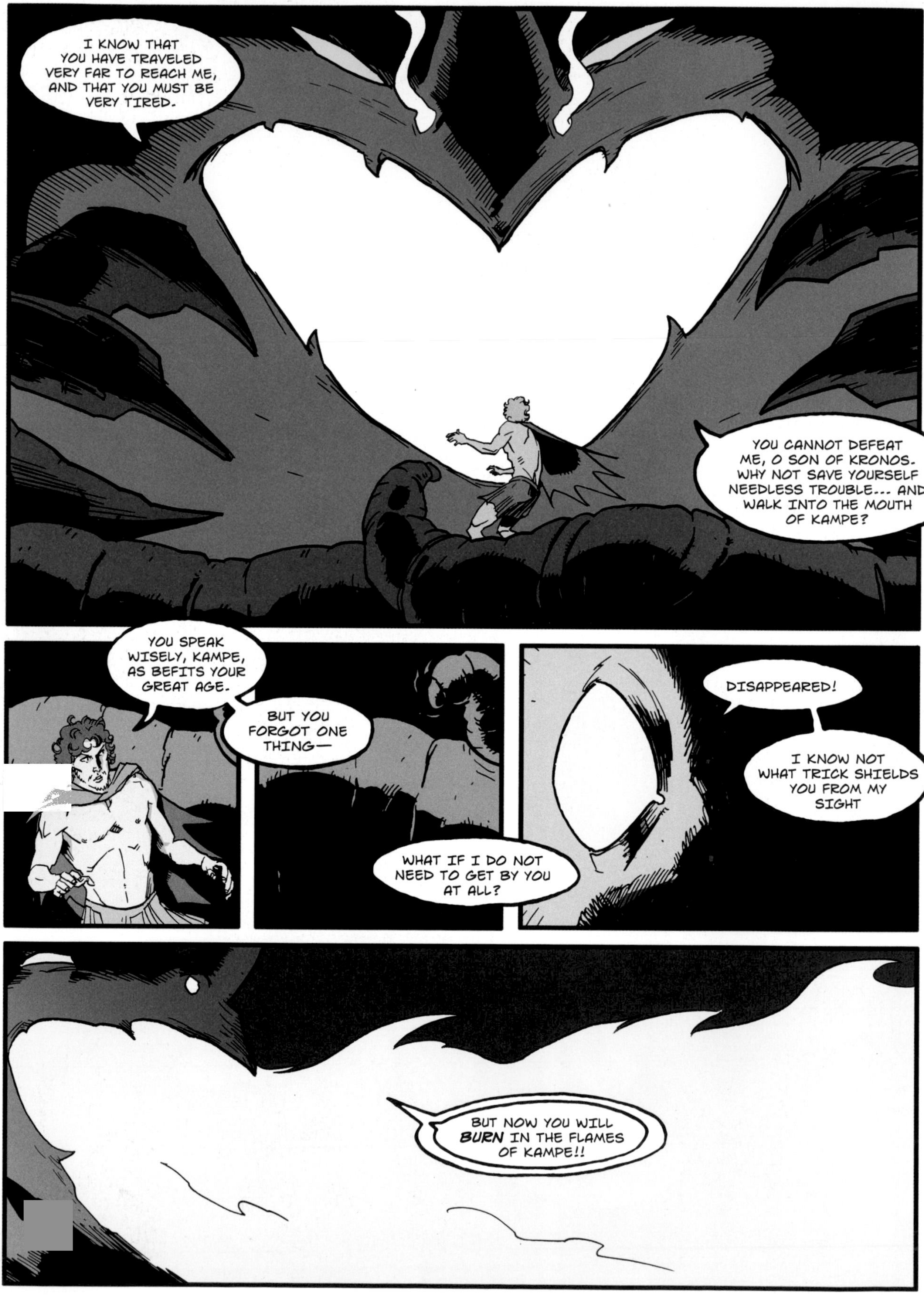
I KNOW THAT YOU HAVE TRAVELED VERY FAR TO REACH ME, AND THAT YOU MUST BE VERY TIRED.
YOU CANNOT DEFEAT ME, O SON OF KRONOS. WHY NOT SAVE YOURSELF NEEDLESS TROUBLE... AND WALK INTO THE MOUTH OF KAMPE?
YOU SPEAK WISELY, KAMPE, AS BEFITS YOUR GREAT AGE.
BUT YOU FORGOT ONE THING—
WHAT IF I DO NOT NEED TO GET BY YOU AT ALL?
DISAPPEARED!
I KNOW NOT WHAT TRICK SHIELDS YOU FROM MY SIGHT
BUT NOW YOU WILL BURN IN THE FLAMES OF KAMPE!!

YOU CANNOT BURN WHAT YOU CANNOT TOUCH, KAMPE, AND YOU CAN NO LONGER TOUCH ME.

WHAT?!

I AM INVISIBLE, IMMATERIAL!

TRICKERY!

OR PERHAPS IT IS YOUR AGE WHICH BETRAYS YOU, O GREAT KAMPE.

AND YOU CAN NO LONGER SEE THAT WHICH IS BEFORE YOUR VERY SNOUT!

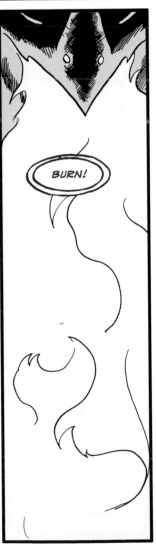

BURN!

BURN!!

BUR—WHAT?

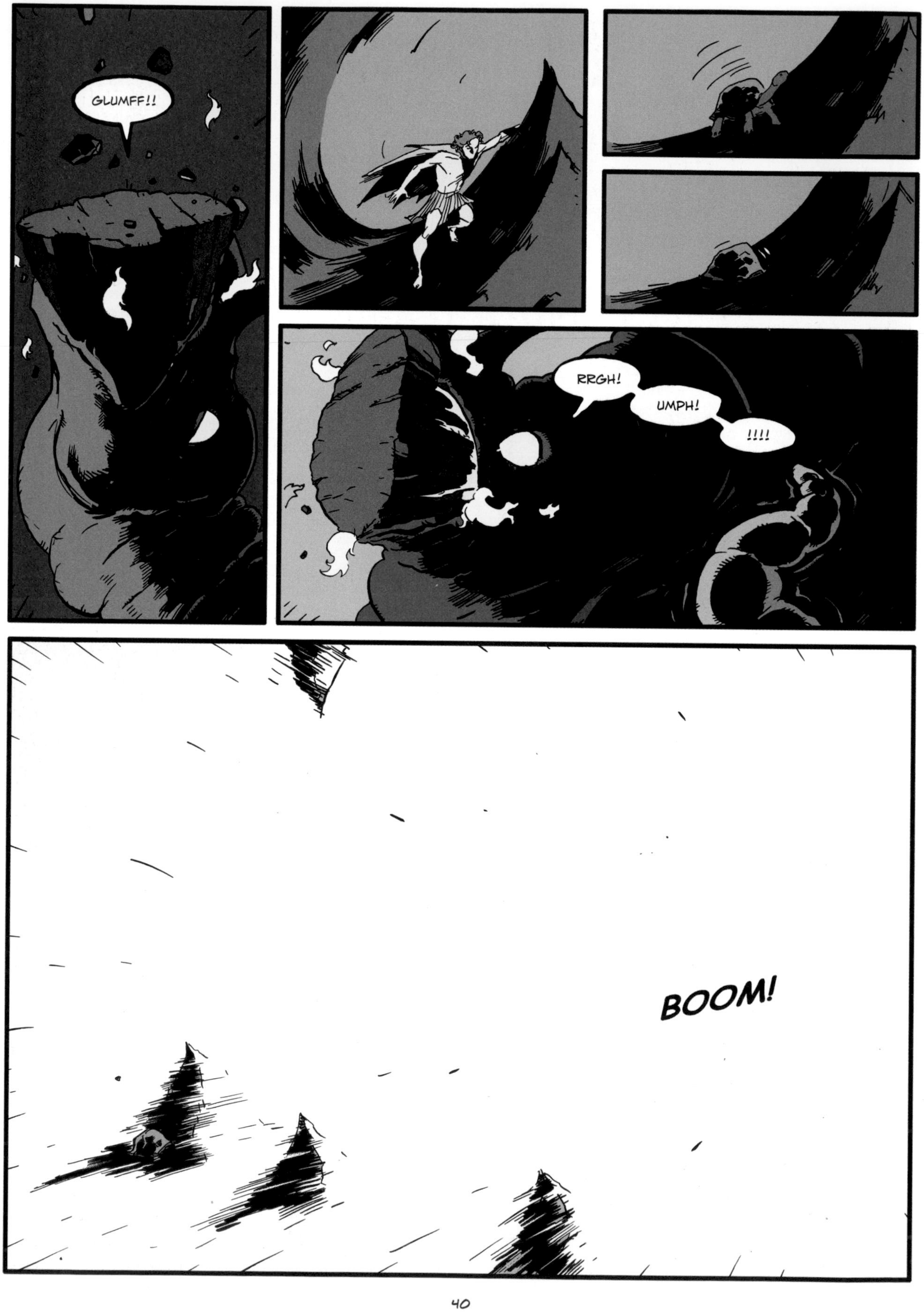
GLUMFF!!
RRGH!
UMPH!
!!!!
BOOM!

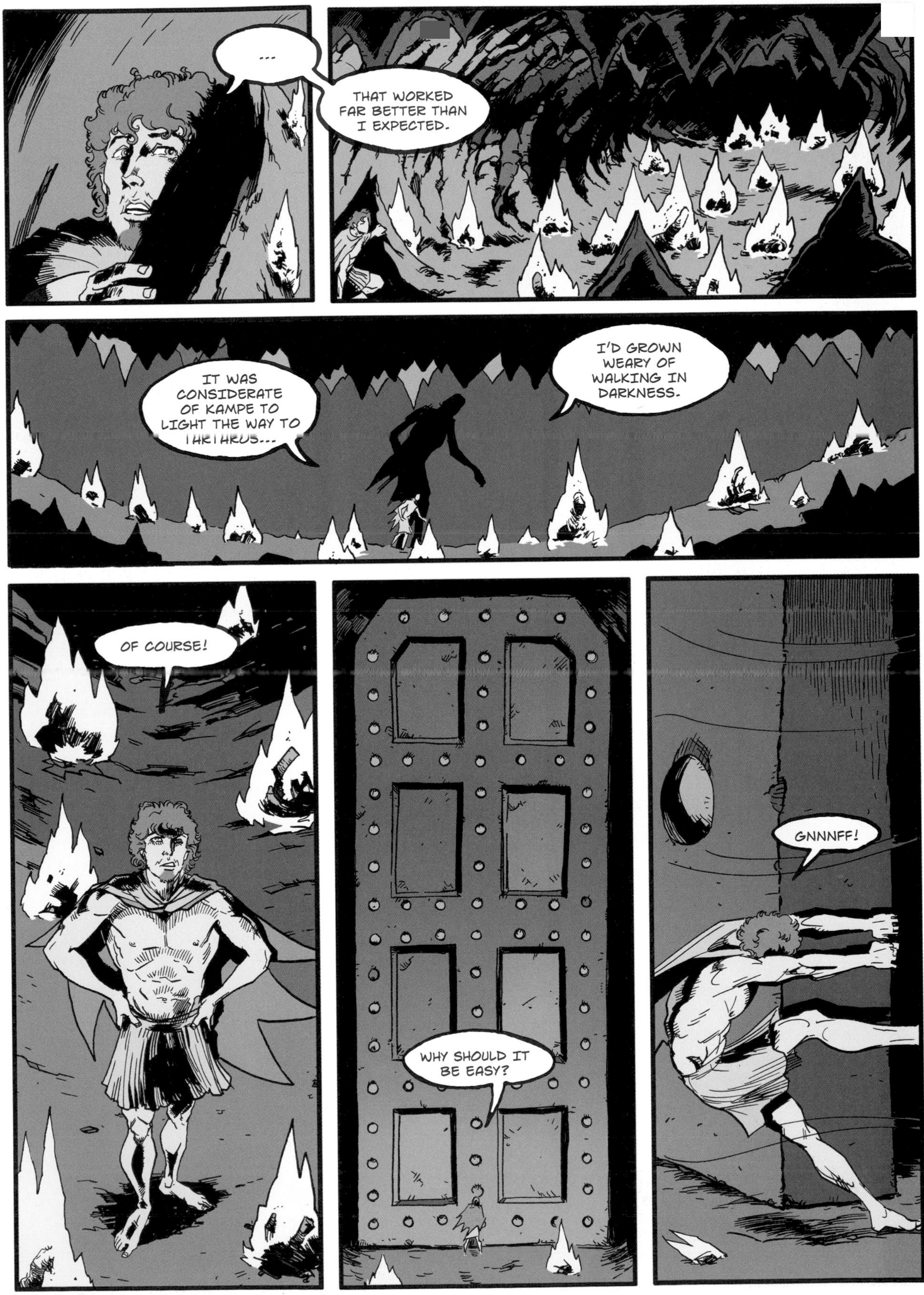
...
THAT WORKED FAR BETTER THAN I EXPECTED.
IT WAS CONSIDERATE OF KAMPE TO LIGHT THE WAY TO TARTARUS...
I'D GROWN WEARY OF WALKING IN DARKNESS.
OF COURSE!
WHY SHOULD IT BE EASY?
GNNNFF!

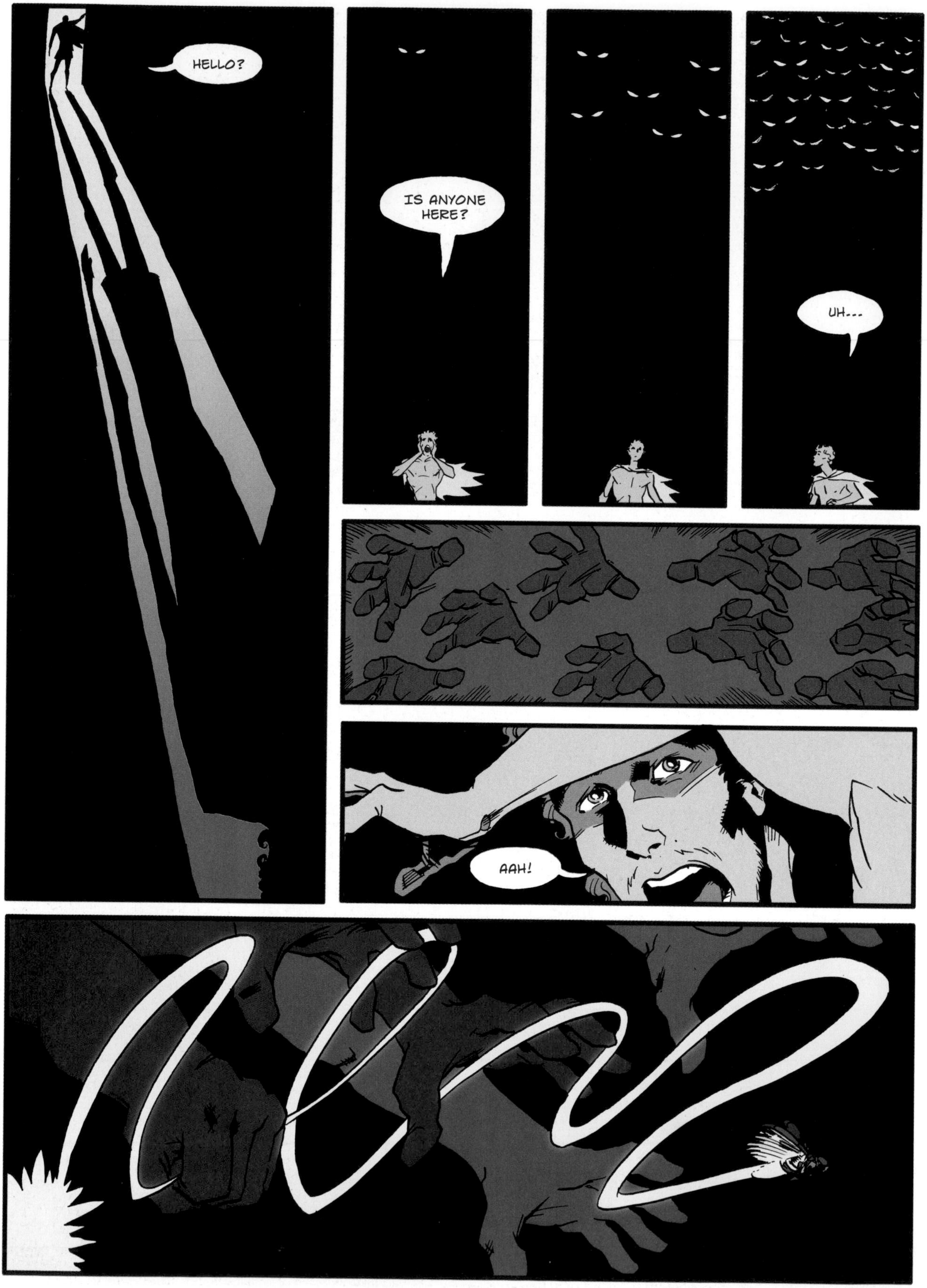
HELLO?
IS ANYONE HERE?
UH...
AAH!

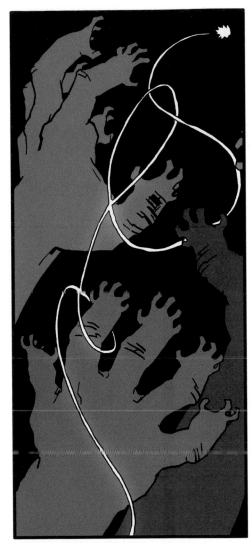
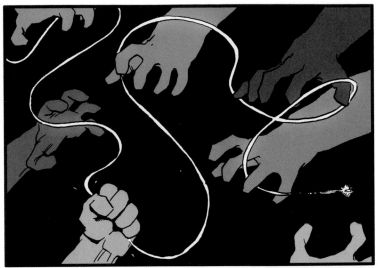
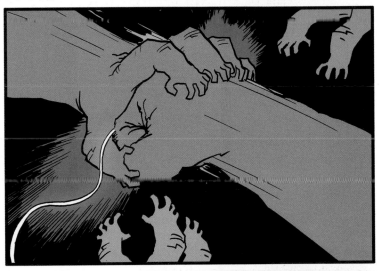

RUH?

SQUEE!

SQUEEE!!

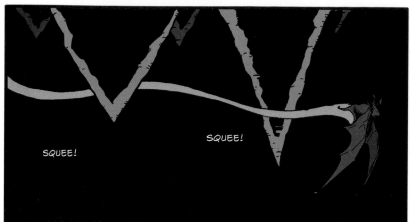

SQUEE!

SQUEE!

OOF!

UNH...

AH.

BEHOLD, MY BROTHERS. IT SEEMS THAT WE HAVE A VISITOR.

IT'S BEEN A VERY, VERY LONG TIME SINCE WE'VE HAD VISITORS IN TARTAROS.

ANNOUNCE YOURSELF.

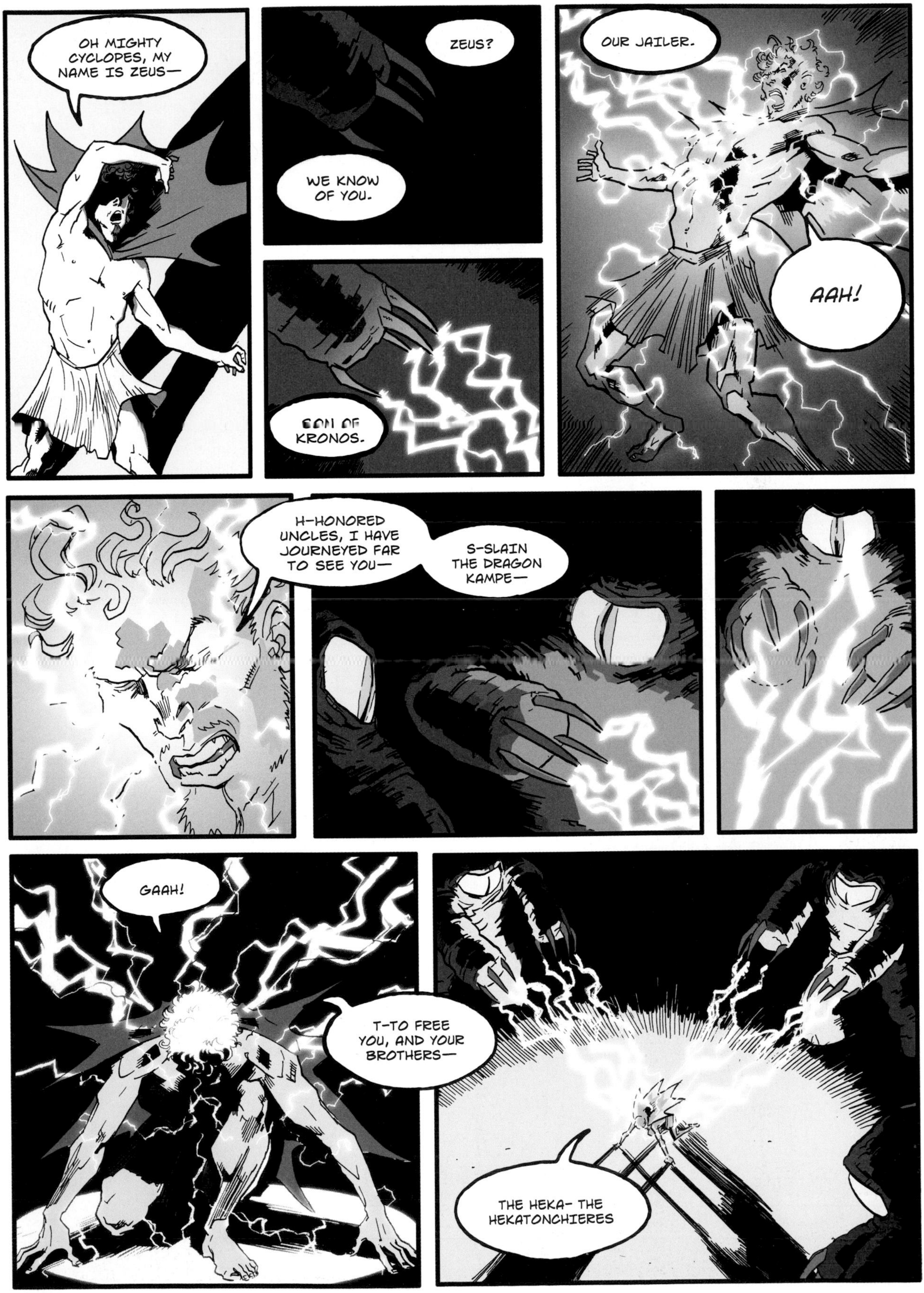
OH MIGHTY CYCLOPES, MY NAME IS ZEUS—
ZEUS?
WE KNOW OF YOU.
SON OF KRONOS.
OUR JAILER.
AAH!
H-HONORED UNCLES, I HAVE JOURNEYED FAR TO SEE YOU—
S-SLAIN THE DRAGON KAMPE—
GAAH!
T-TO FREE YOU, AND YOUR BROTHERS—
THE HEKA- THE HEKATONCHIERES

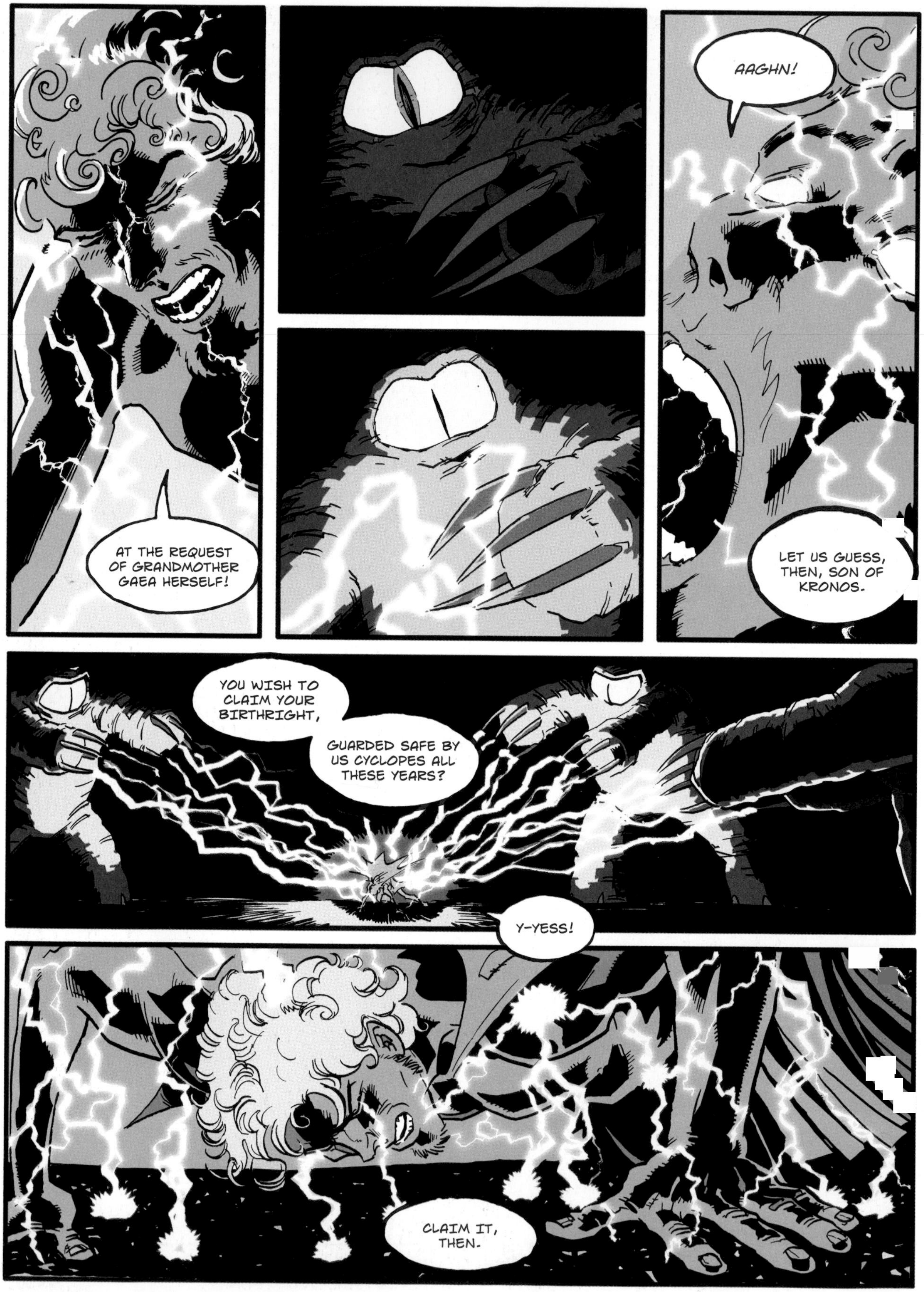
AT THE REQUEST OF GRANDMOTHER GAEA HERSELF!
AAGHN!
LET US GUESS, THEN, SON OF KRONOS.
YOU WISH TO CLAIM YOUR BIRTHRIGHT,
GUARDED SAFE BY US CYCLOPES ALL THESE YEARS?
Y-YESS!
CLAIM IT, THEN.

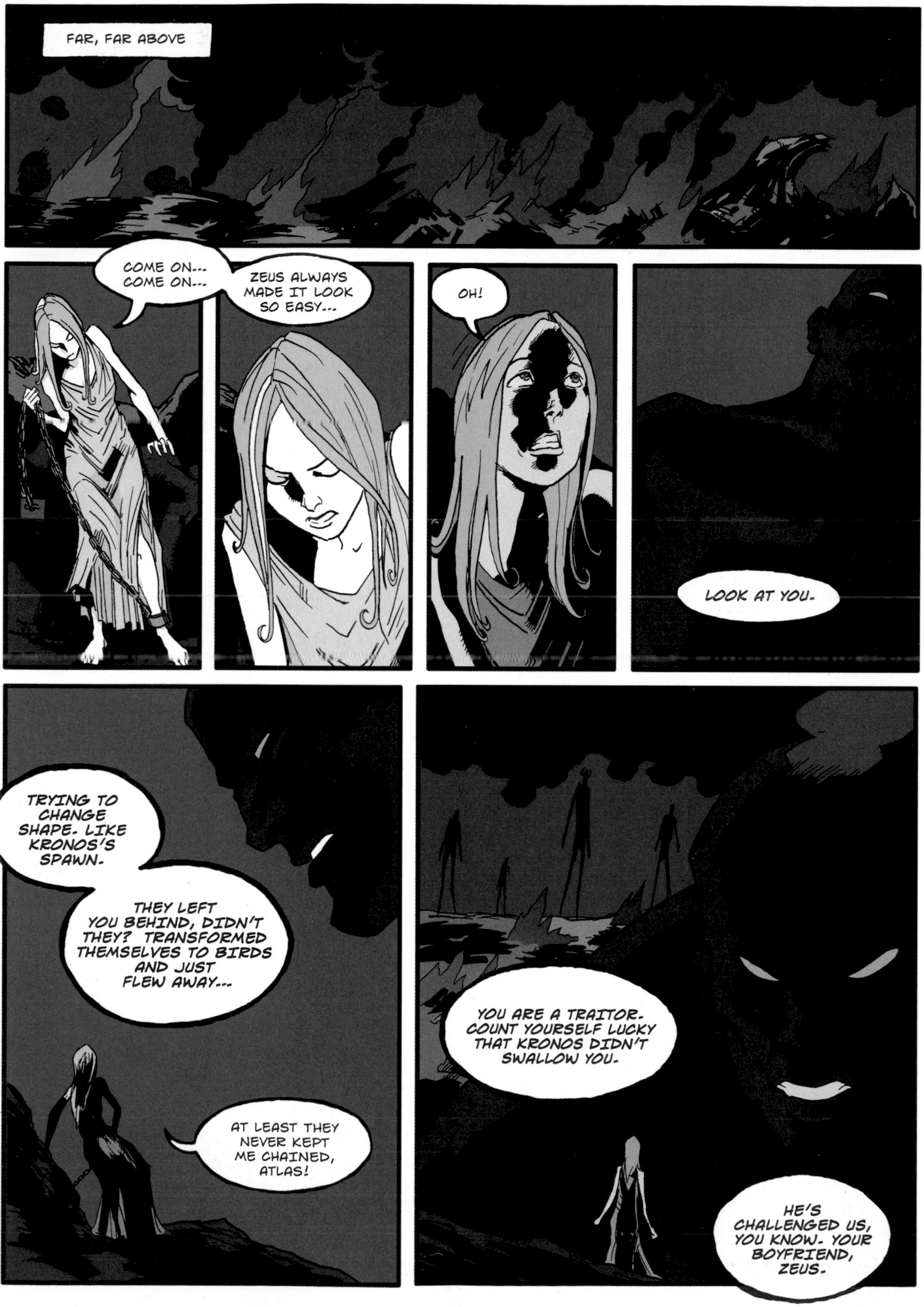
FAR, FAR ABOVE
COME ON... COME ON...
ZEUS ALWAYS MADE IT LOOK SO EASY...
OH!
LOOK AT YOU.
TRYING TO CHANGE SHAPE. LIKE KRONOS'S SPAWN.
THEY LEFT YOU BEHIND, DIDN'T THEY? TRANSFORMED THEMSELVES TO BIRDS AND JUST FLEW AWAY...
AT LEAST THEY NEVER KEPT ME CHAINED, ATLAS!
YOU ARE A TRAITOR. COUNT YOURSELF LUCKY THAT KRONOS DIDN'T SWALLOW YOU.
HE'S CHALLENGED US, YOU KNOW. YOUR BOYFRIEND, ZEUS.

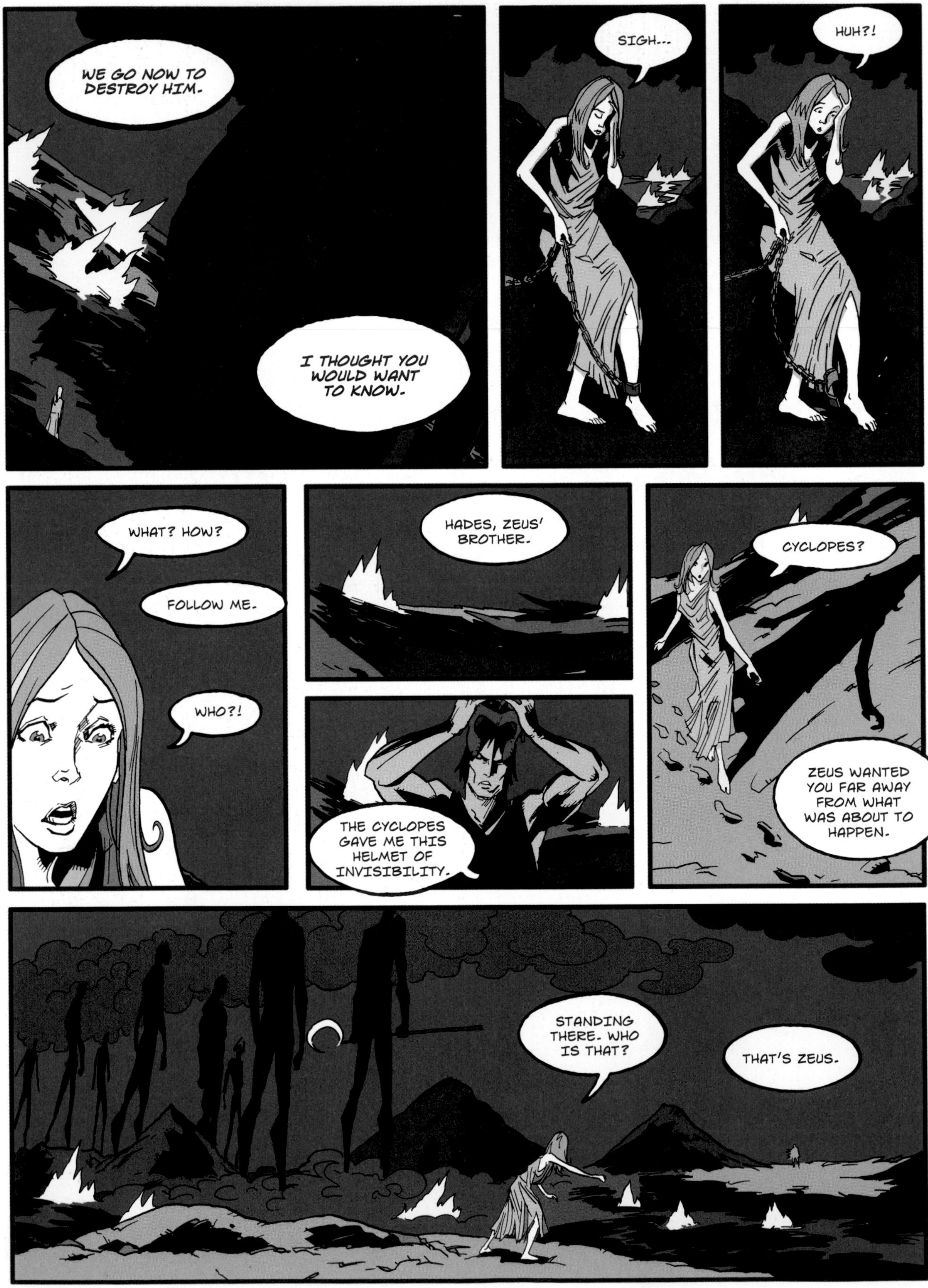
WE GO NOW TO DESTROY HIM.
I THOUGHT YOU WOULD WANT TO KNOW.
SIGH...
HUH?!
WHAT? HOW?
FOLLOW ME.
WHO?!
HADES, ZEUS' BROTHER.
THE CYCLOPES GAVE ME THIS HELMET OF INVISIBILITY.
CYCLOPES?
ZEUS WANTED YOU FAR AWAY FROM WHAT WAS ABOUT TO HAPPEN.
STANDING THERE. WHO IS THAT?
THAT'S ZEUS.

ZEUS? WHAT DOES HE THINK HE'S DOING?

HE JUST STANDS THERE, AS IF WAITING FOR SOMETHING.

DESTROY HIM.

SON OF KRONOS.

VERY WELL, THEN.

ANYTHING TO SAY FOR YOURSELF?

NO?

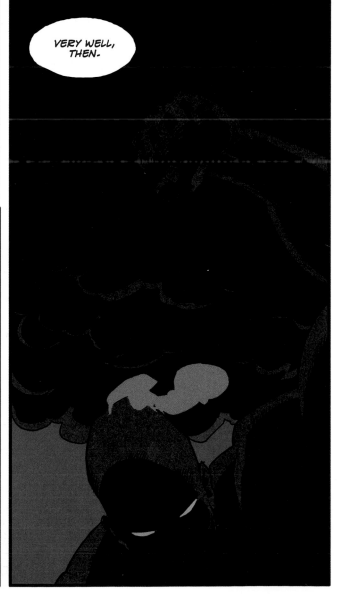

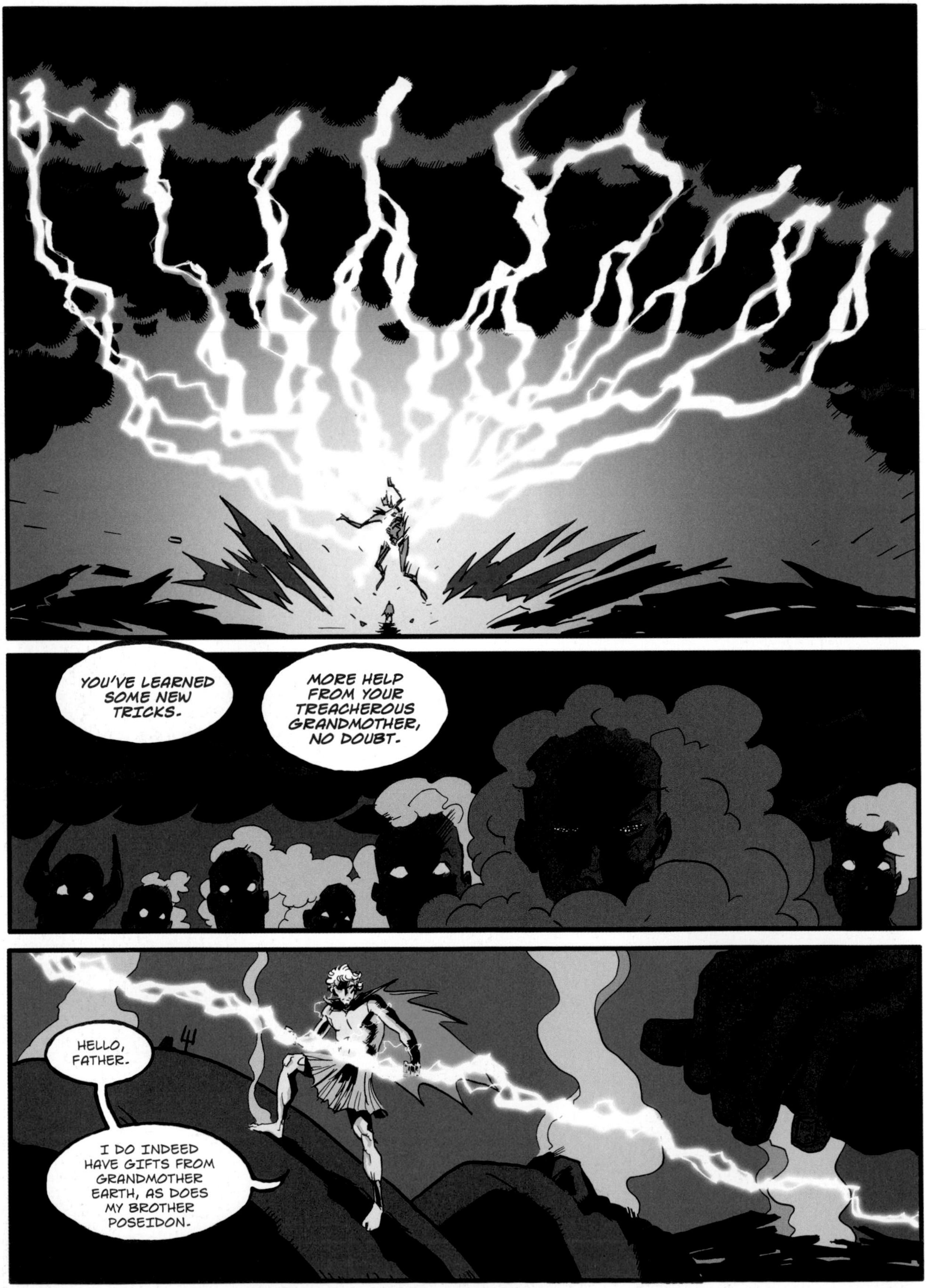
YOU'VE LEARNED SOME NEW TRICKS.
MORE HELP FROM YOUR TREACHEROUS GRANDMOTHER, NO DOUBT.
HELLO, FATHER.
I DO INDEED HAVE GIFTS FROM GRANDMOTHER EARTH, AS DOES MY BROTHER POSEIDON.

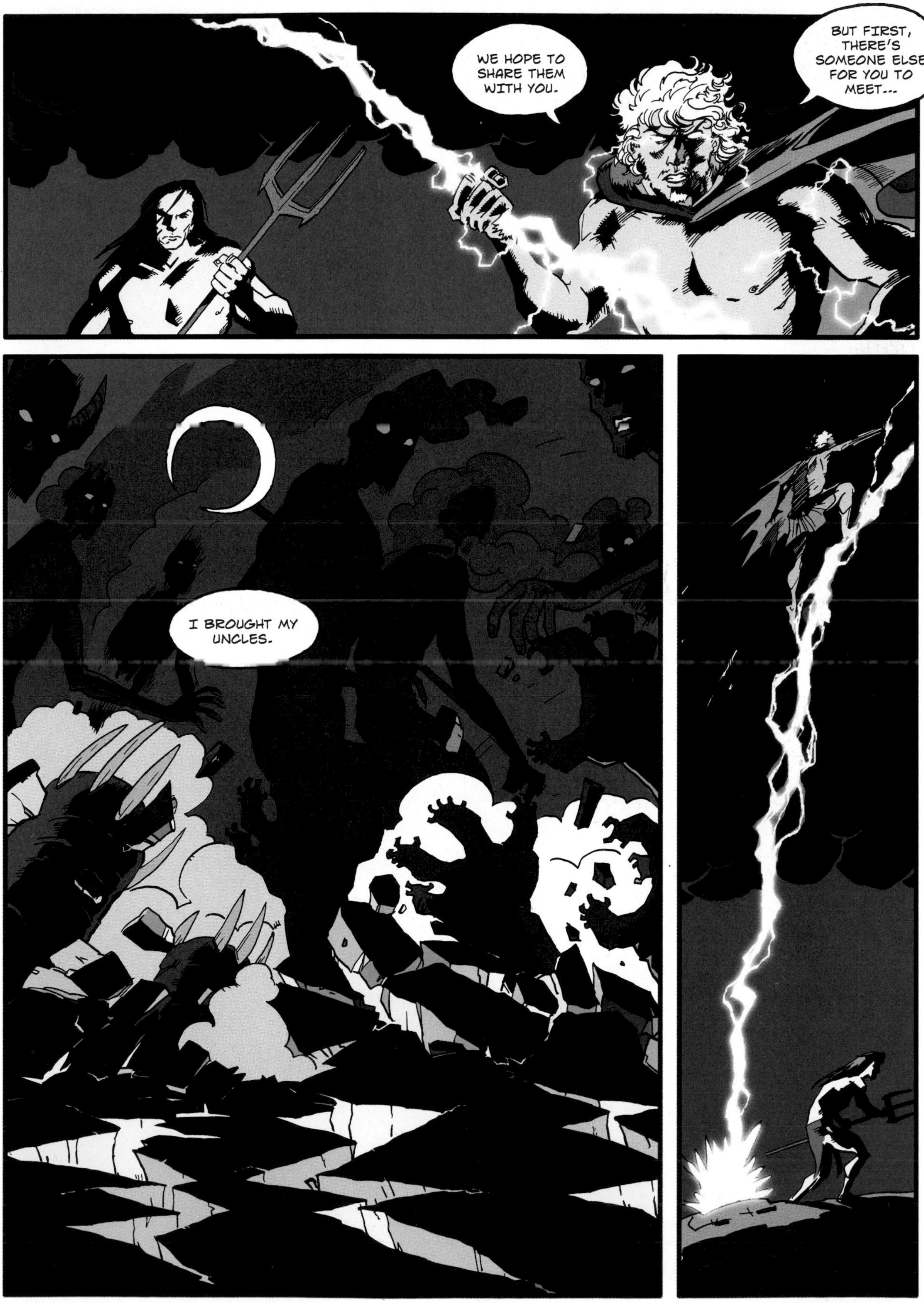
WE HOPE TO SHARE THEM WITH YOU.
BUT FIRST, THERE'S SOMEONE ELSE FOR YOU TO MEET...
I BROUGHT MY UNCLES.

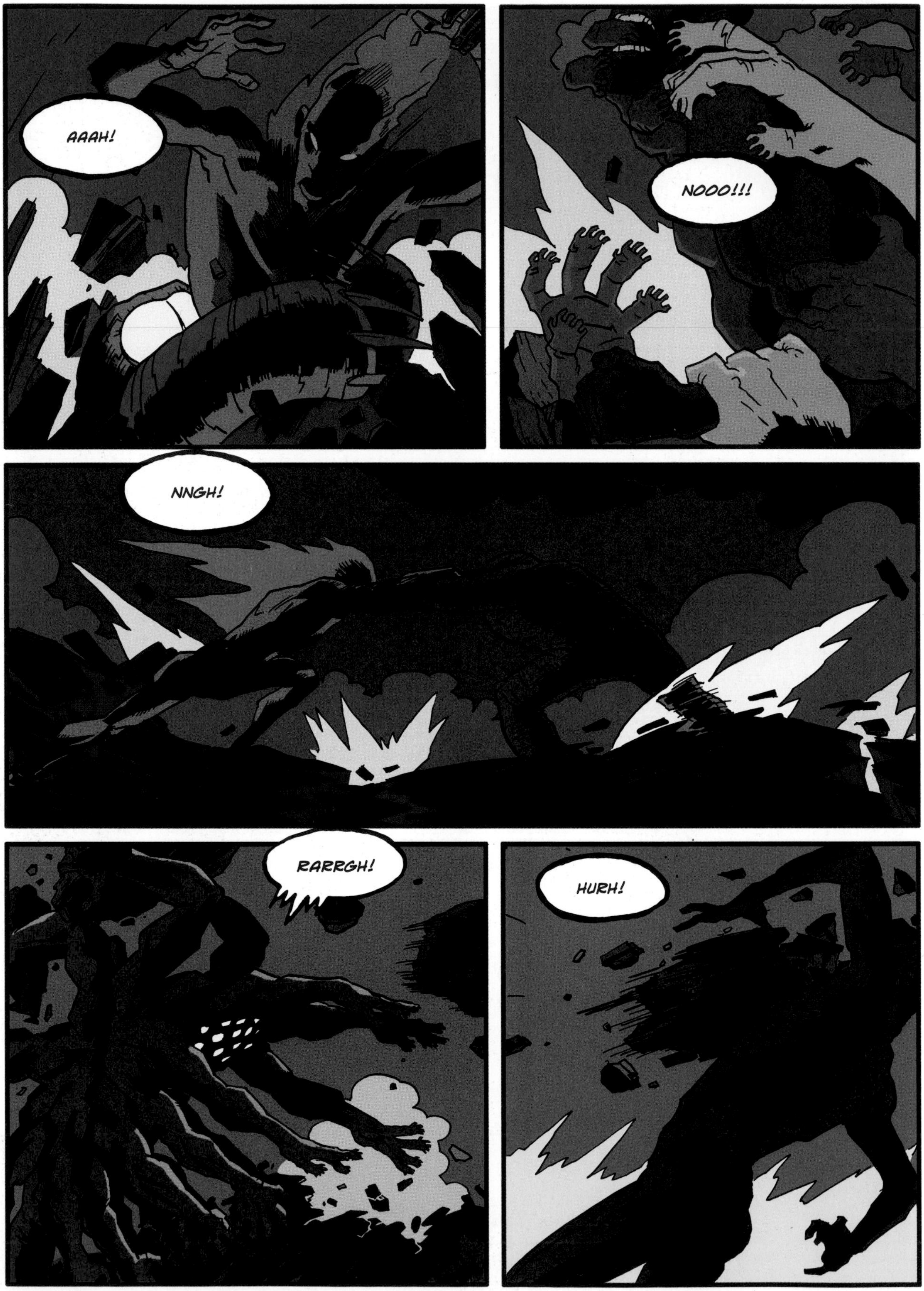
AAAH!
NOOO!!!
NNGH!
RARRGH!
HURH!

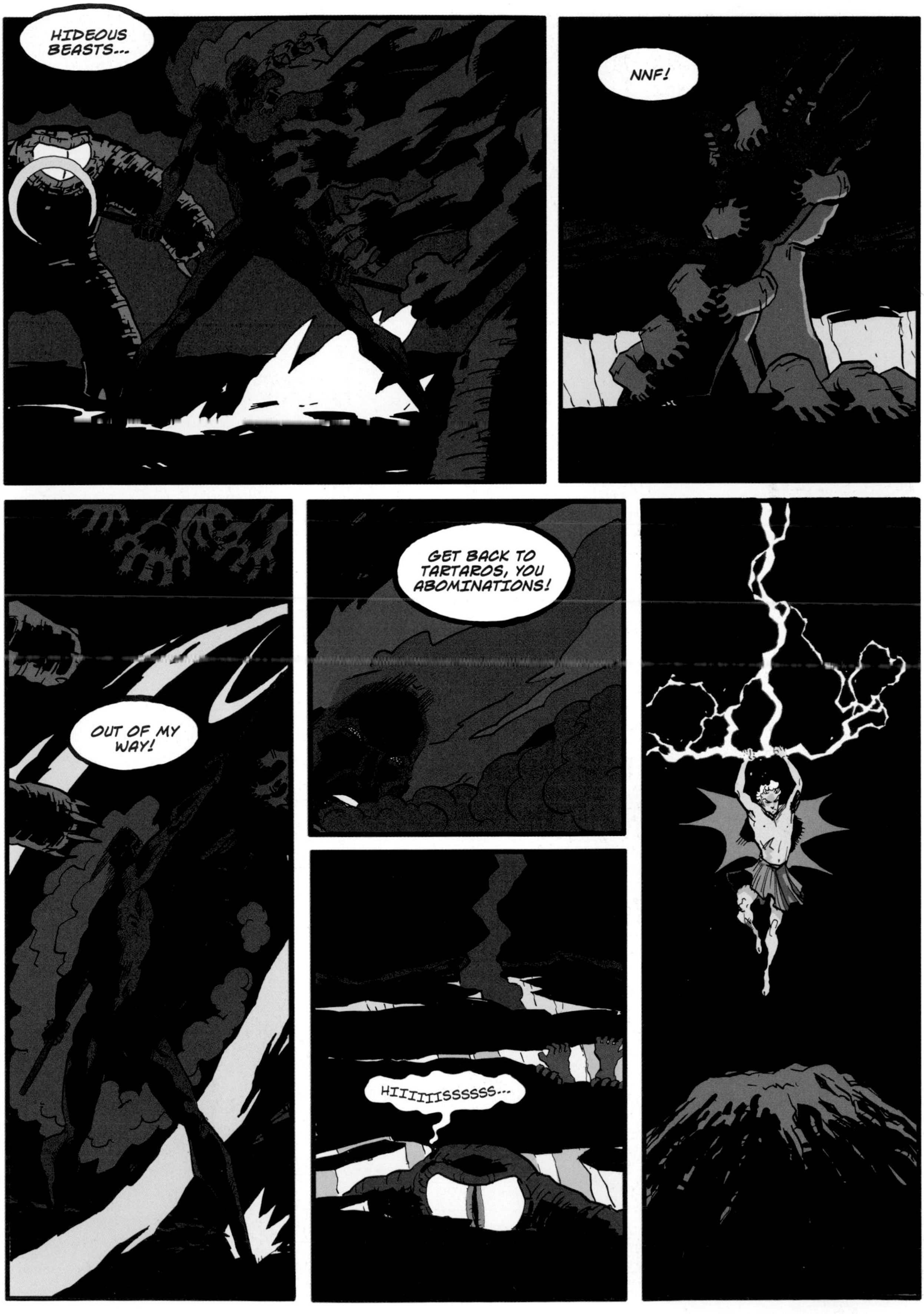
HIDEOUS BEASTS...
NNF!
OUT OF MY WAY!
GET BACK TO TARTAROS, YOU ABOMINATIONS!
HIIIIIIISSSSSS...

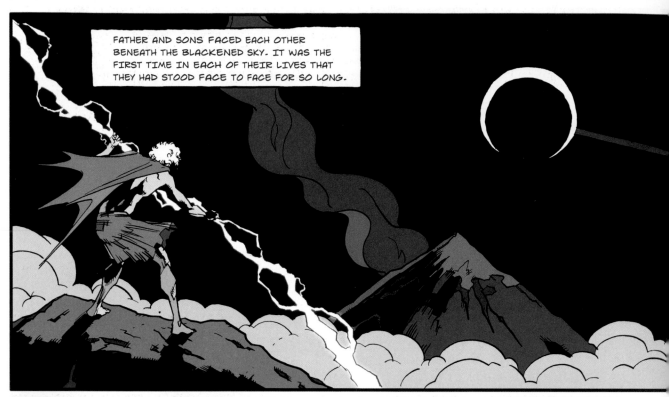

FATHER AND SONS FACED EACH OTHER BENEATH THE BLACKENED SKY. IT WAS THE FIRST TIME IN EACH OF THEIR LIVES THAT THEY HAD STOOD FACE TO FACE FOR SO LONG.

HAH!

HURNH.

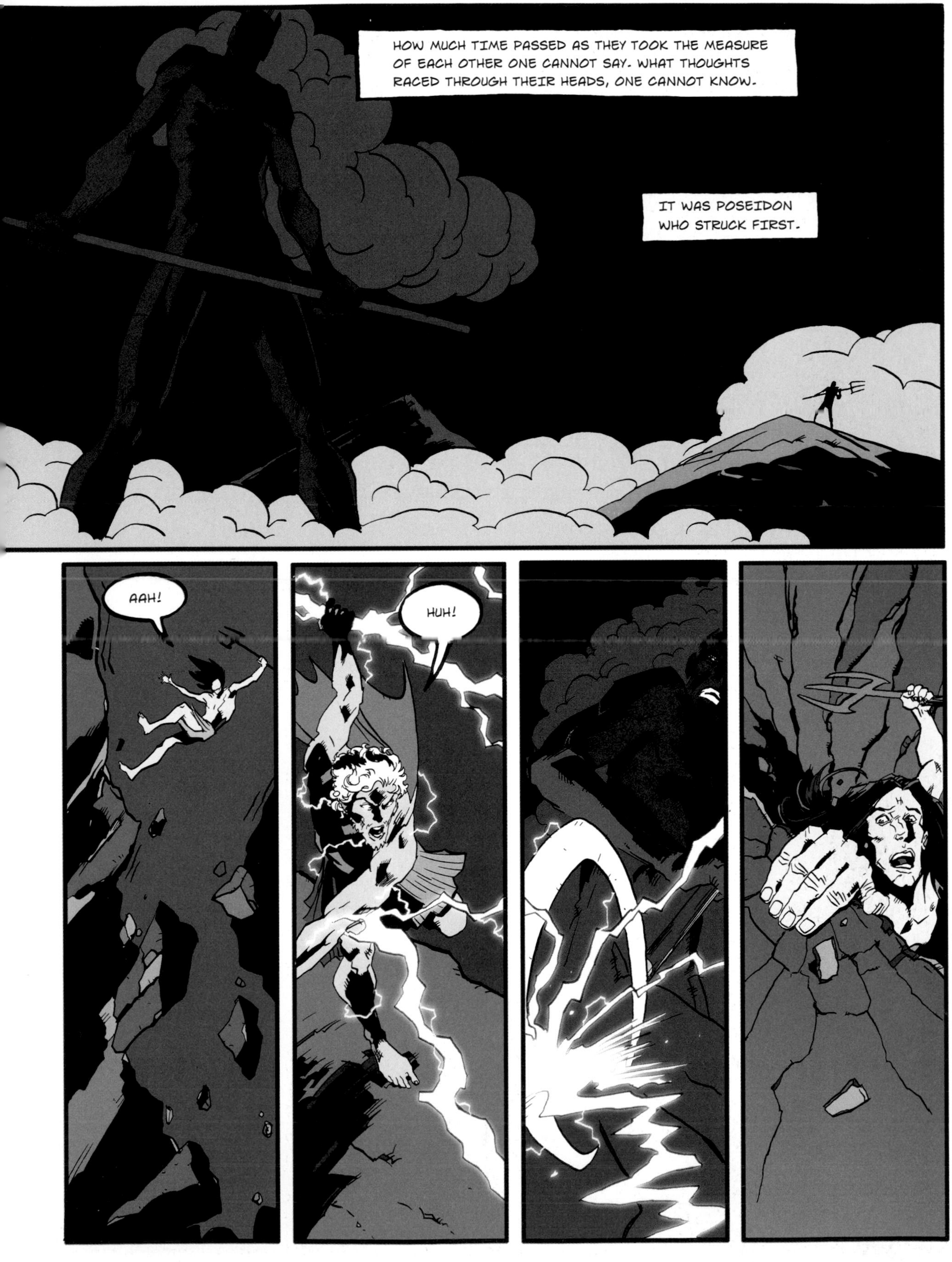
HOW MUCH TIME PASSED AS THEY TOOK THE MEASURE OF EACH OTHER ONE CANNOT SAY. WHAT THOUGHTS RACED THROUGH THEIR HEADS, ONE CANNOT KNOW.
IT WAS POSEIDON WHO STRUCK FIRST.
AAH!
HUH!

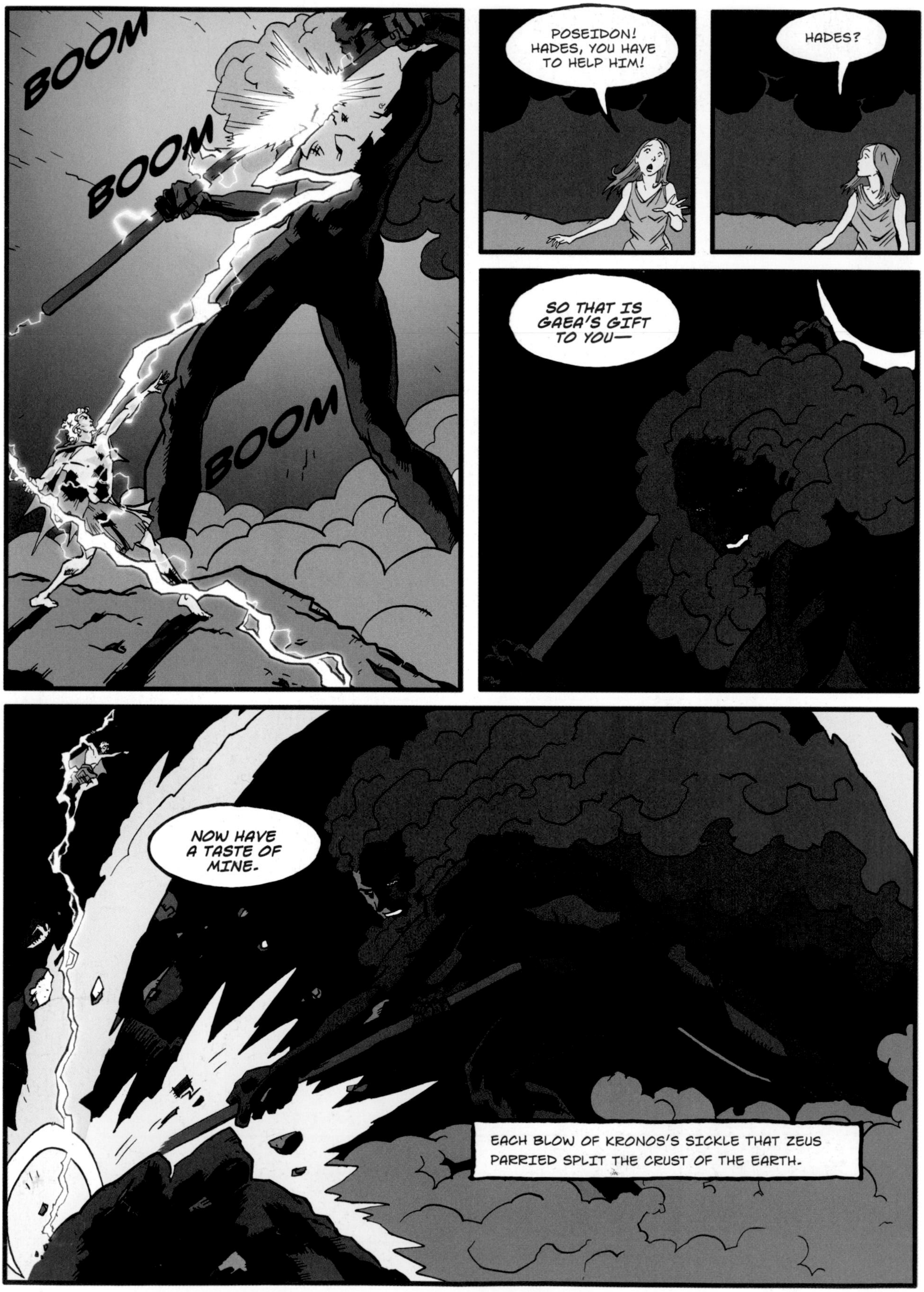
BOOM
BOOM
BOOM
POSEIDON! HADES, YOU HAVE TO HELP HIM!
HADES?
SO THAT IS GAEA'S GIFT TO YOU—
NOW HAVE A TASTE OF MINE.
EACH BLOW OF KRONOS'S SICKLE THAT ZEUS PARRIED SPLIT THE CRUST OF THE EARTH.

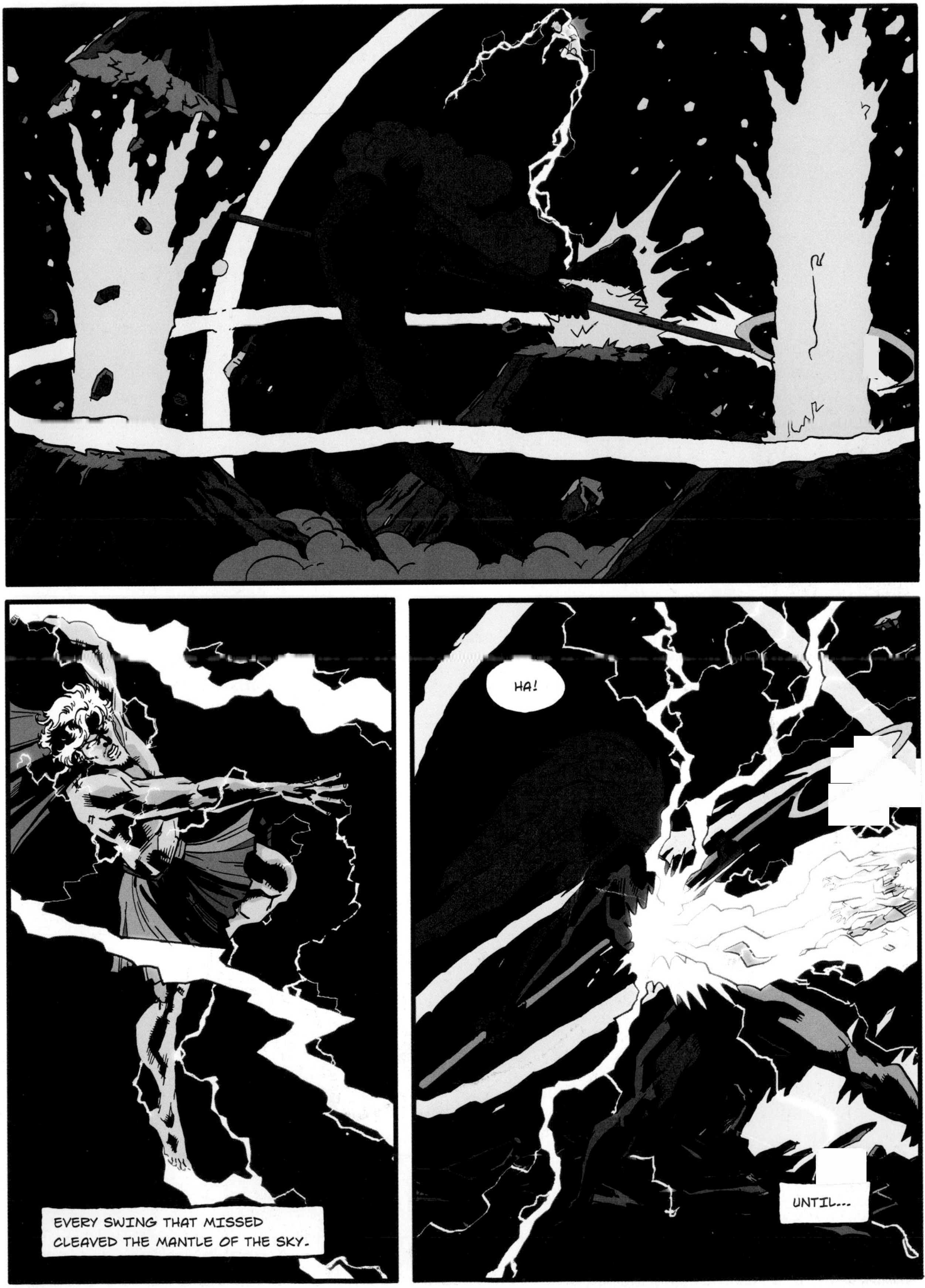
EVERY SWING THAT MISSED
CLEAVED THE MANTLE OF THE SKY.
HA!
UNTIL...

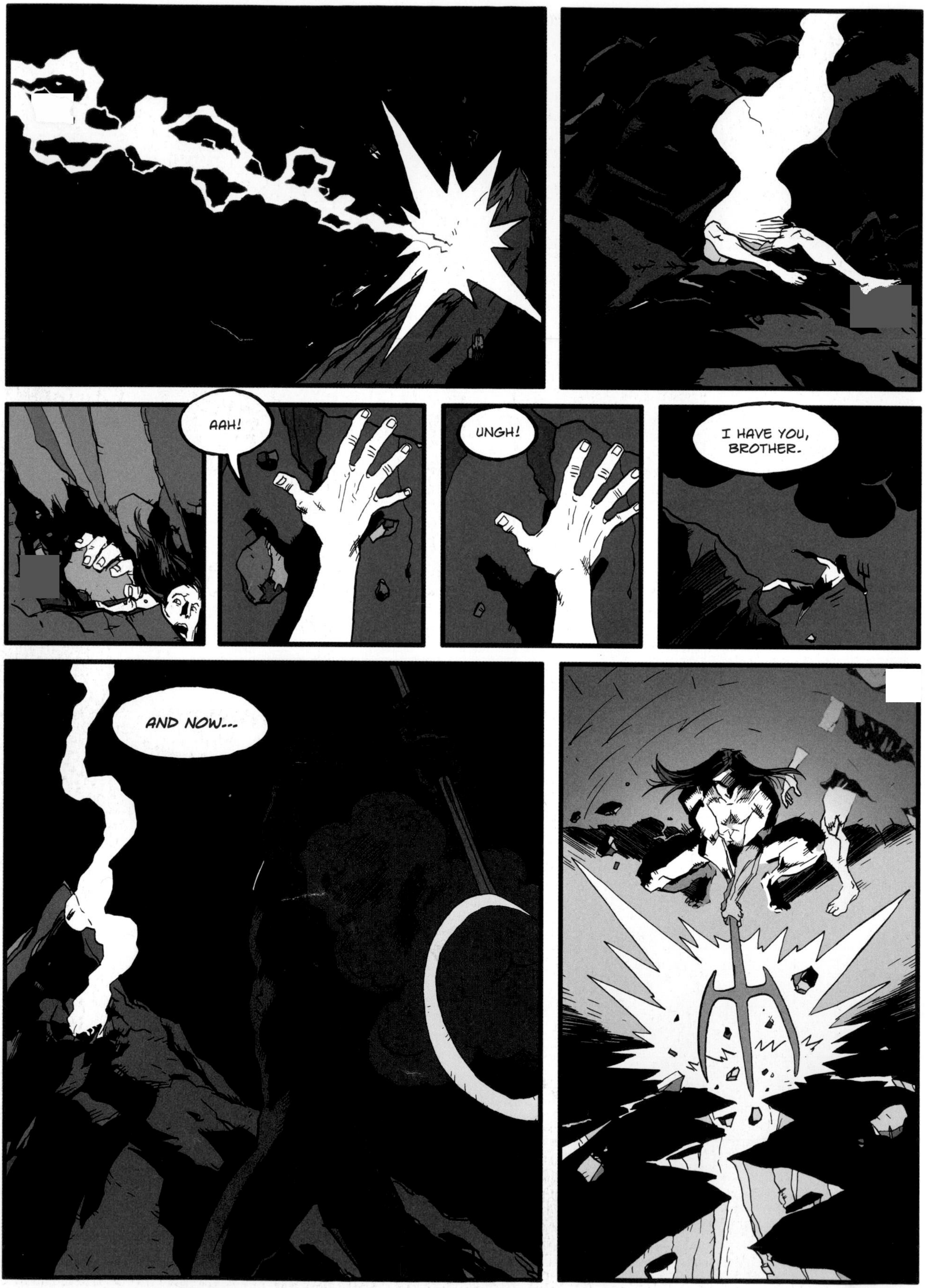
AAH!
UNGH!
I HAVE YOU, BROTHER.
AND NOW...

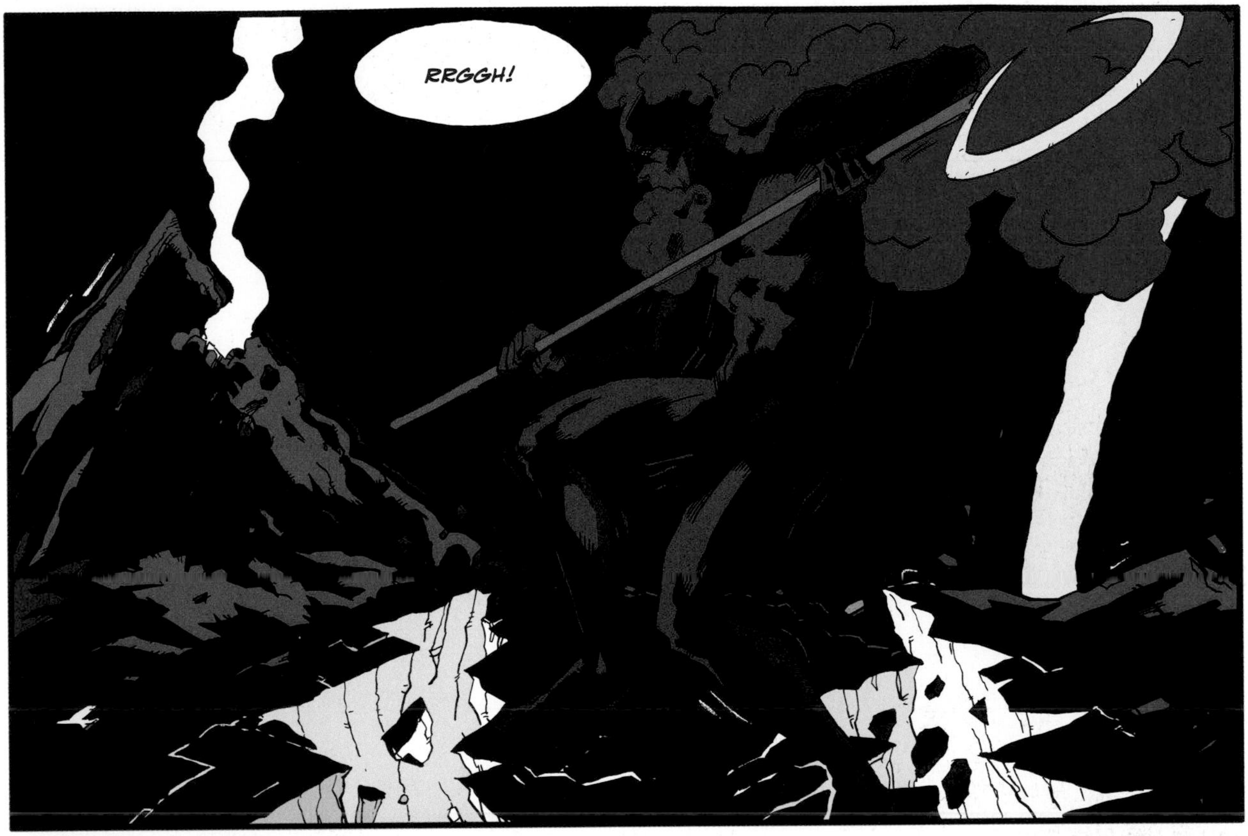
RRGGH!

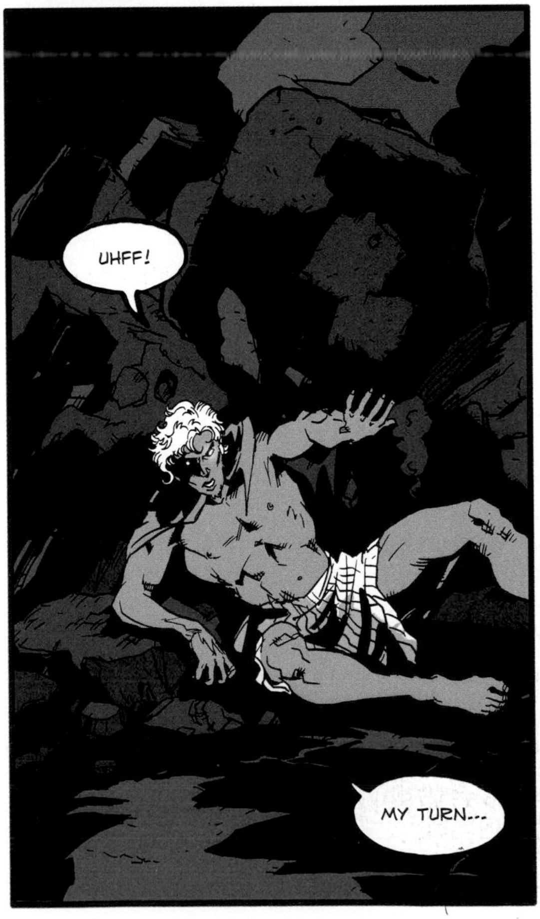
UHFF!
MY TURN...

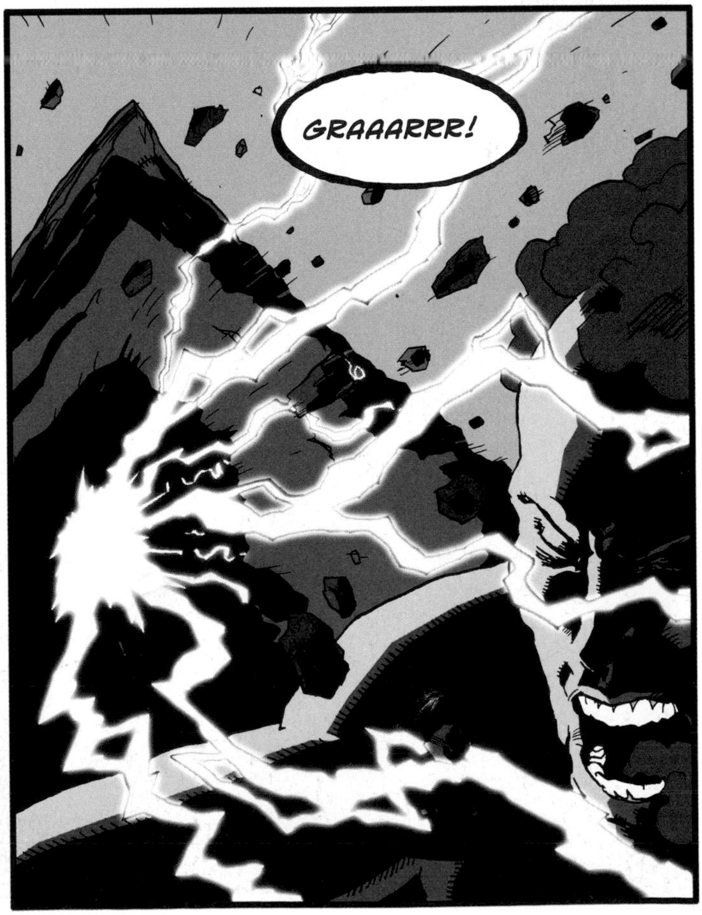
GRAAARRR!

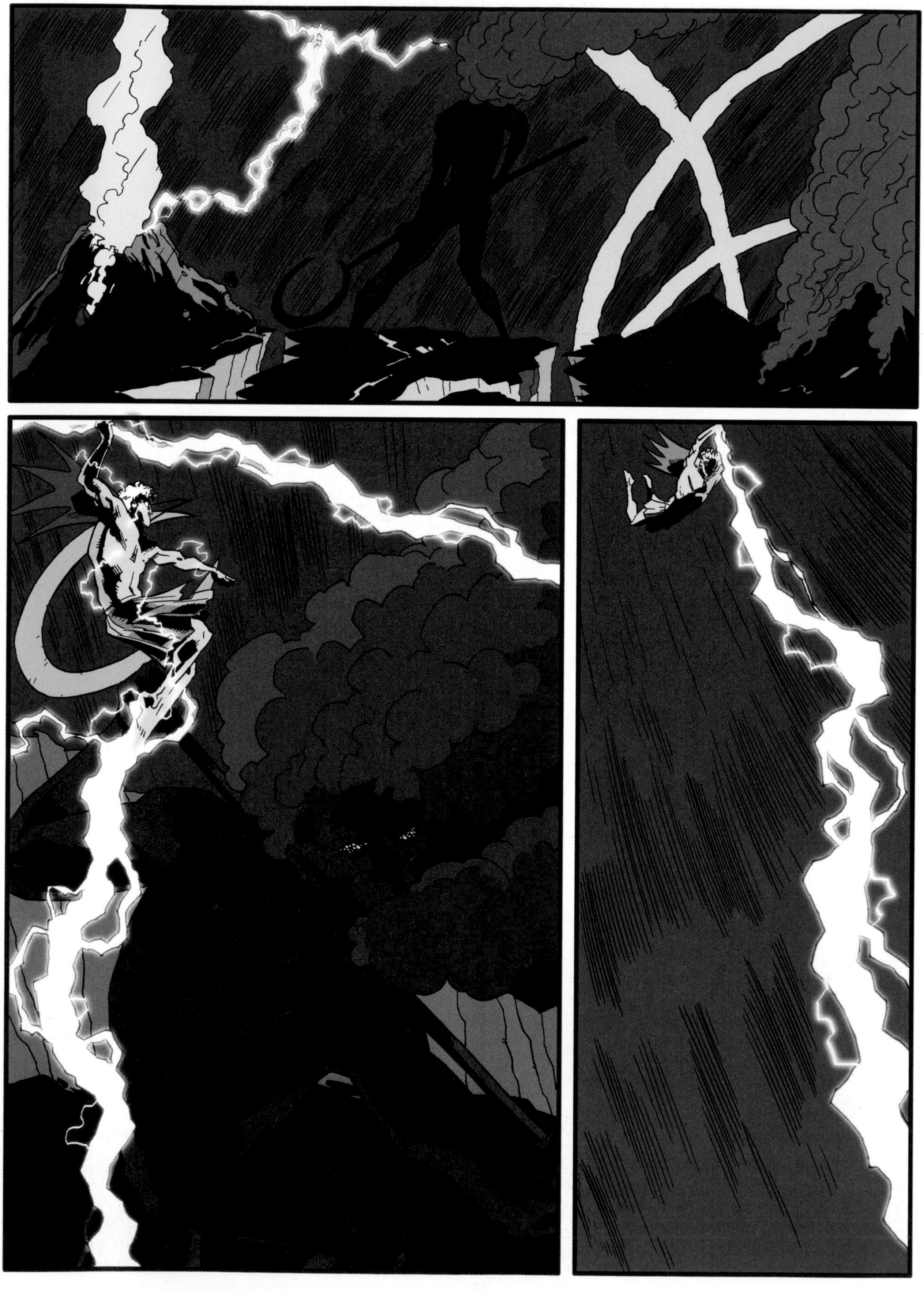

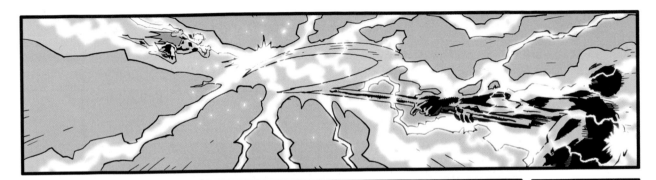

BOOM!

HUNH!

MY...MY SICKLE...
WHERE?...

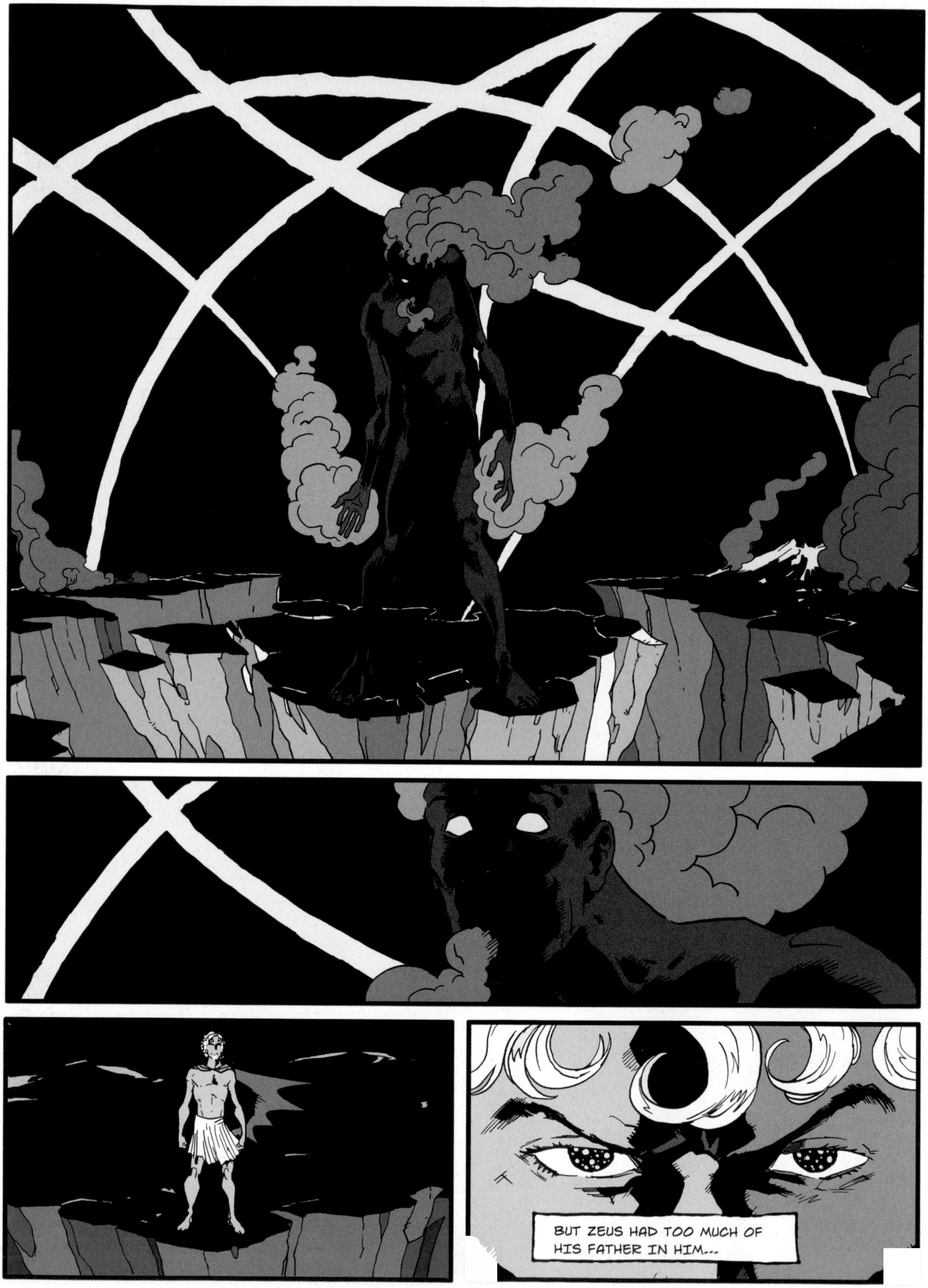
BUT ZEUS HAD TOO MUCH OF
HIS FATHER IN HIM...

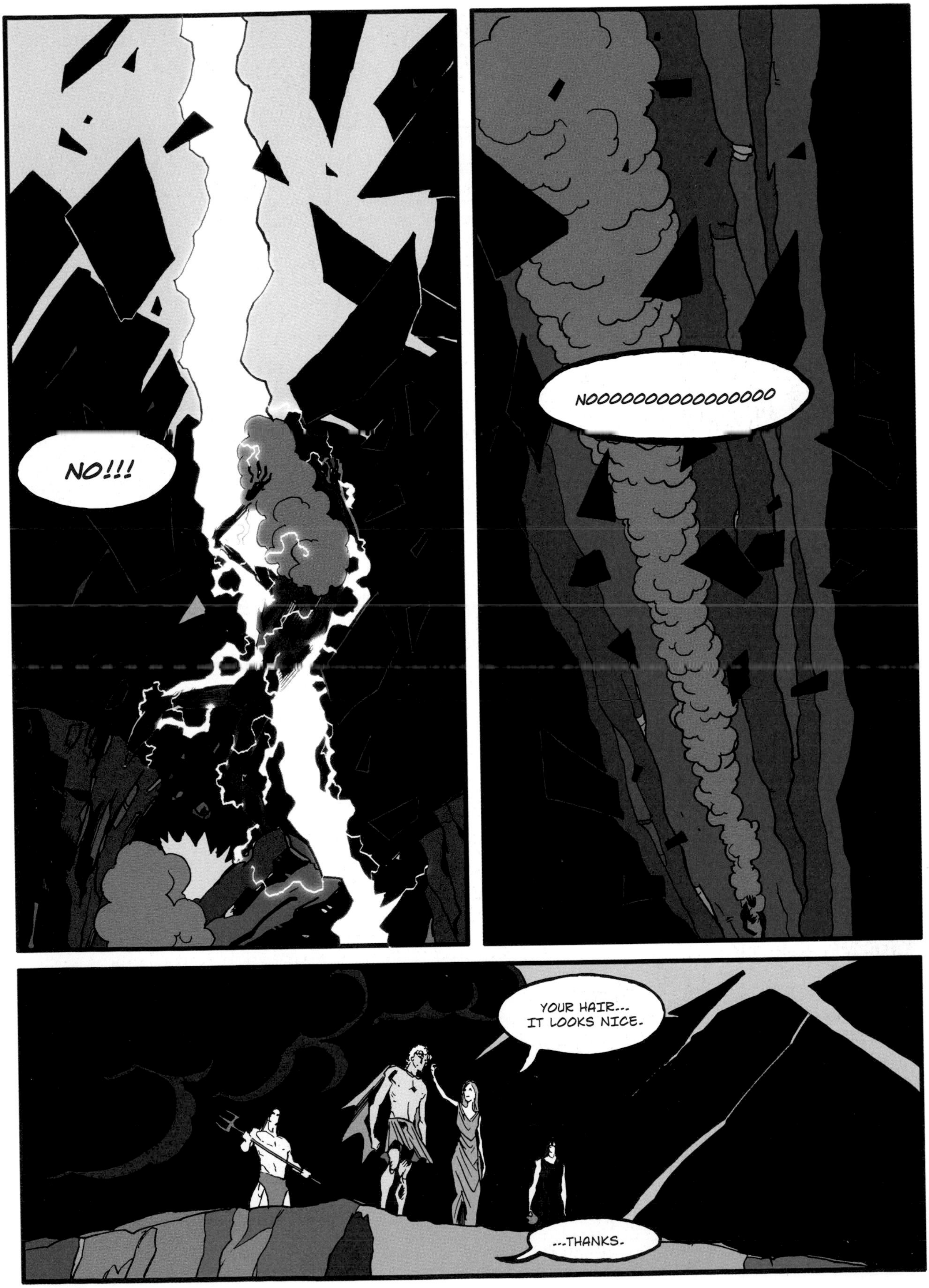
NO!!!
NOOOOOOOOOOOOOOOO
YOUR HAIR...
IT LOOKS NICE.
...THANKS.

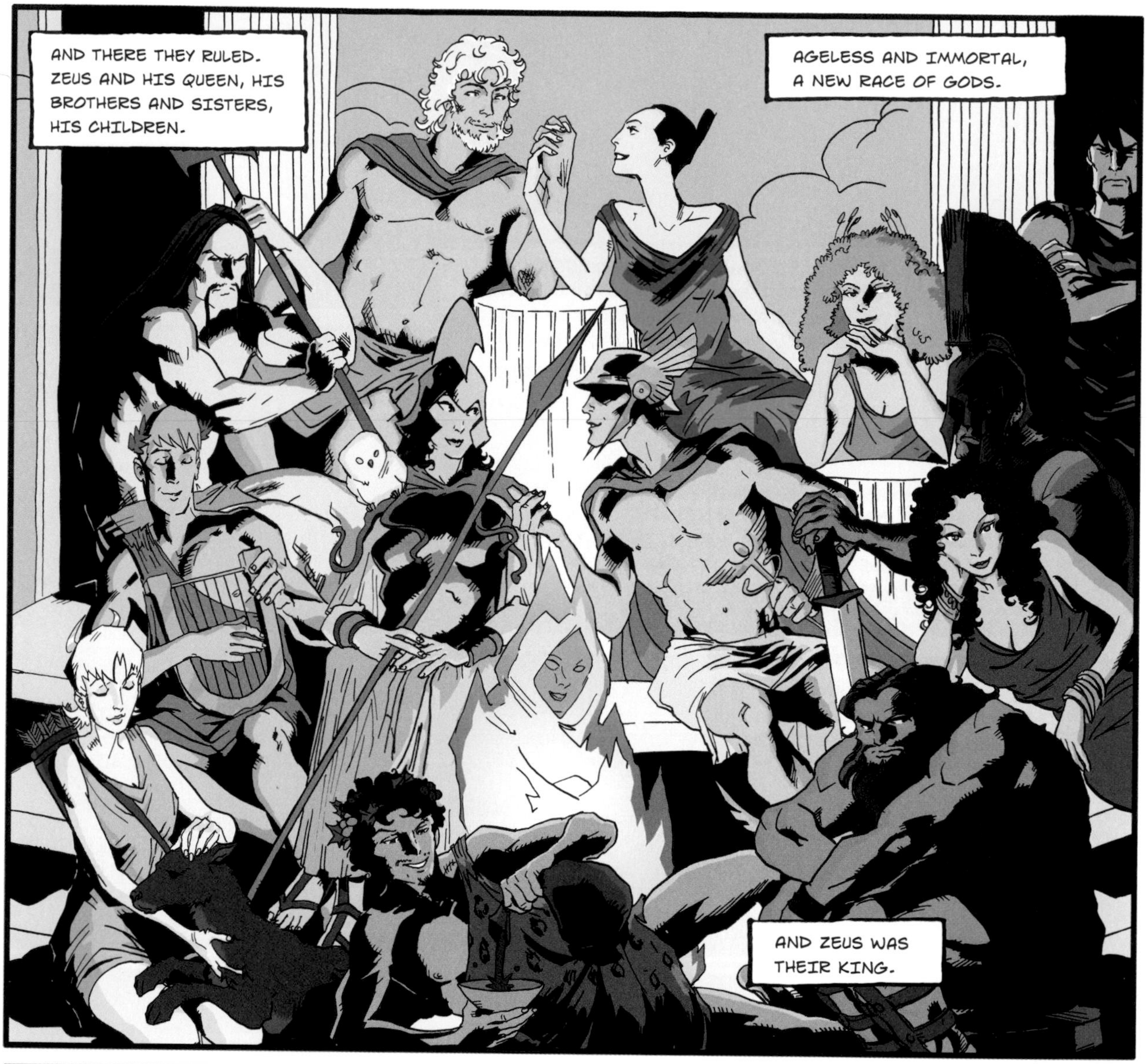
AND THERE THEY RULED. ZEUS AND HIS QUEEN, HIS BROTHERS AND SISTERS, HIS CHILDREN.
AGELESS AND IMMORTAL, A NEW RACE OF GODS.
AND ZEUS WAS THEIR KING.

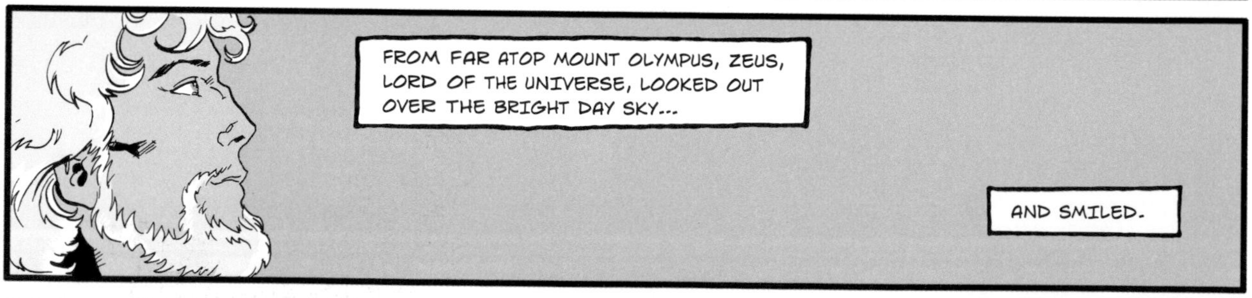
FROM FAR ATOP MOUNT OLYMPUS, ZEUS, LORD OF THE UNIVERSE, LOOKED OUT OVER THE BRIGHT DAY SKY...
AND SMILED.

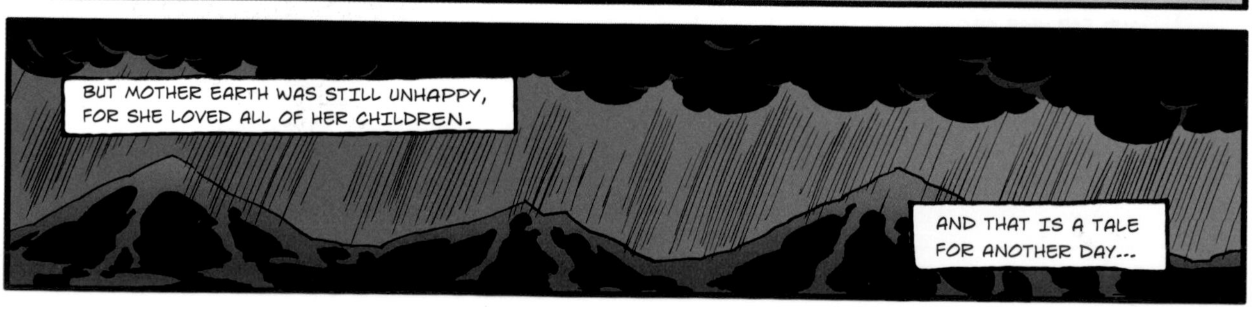
BUT MOTHER EARTH WAS STILL UNHAPPY, FOR SHE LOVED ALL OF HER CHILDREN.
AND THAT IS A TALE FOR ANOTHER DAY...

AUTHOR'S NOTE

Where to start? It began one day, when my editor referred to a mutual acquaintance of ours as Cerberus (the three-headed dog of Hades). I responded with some comment about Cyclopes or Gorgons, and he pulled out an oversized graphic novel from his shelf and said, "How about a book, like this one, retelling the Greek myths?" I went home, and around two weeks later I came back with about two-thirds of the book you're holding, and plans for eleven more.

It began even before that. I was in the sixth grade, and by then I'd read every book in my local library on the Greek and Norse myths. I was home sick from school one day, and my parents brought me a copy of "The Mighty Thor," published by Marvel Comics. The art was weird and wonderful, and I remember staring at it, trying to comprehend whether I loved it or hated it. The story was full of all those enormous, bigger-than-life beasts I remembered from my copy of Edith Hamilton's mythology. I had always loved comics, but that copy of Thor, with its gods and monsters and lightning and drama, changed what comics could be for me.

The stories that make up the body of Greek myths are what remain of an ancient culture's deeply held beliefs. The stories of Zeus and his family are more than just entertaining yarns about giants who slice open the sky and monsters so fearsome their gaze can turn one to stone. They were, and are, an explanation of the world that that ancient culture's people saw around them: a lightning storm could only be the King of Gods hurling his thunderbolt; a volcano could only be the escaped vapors of an entombed Titan.

The Greek myths are very, very old, older than the written word. As such there is no "bible," no one set version of how events had occurred. In the ancient days, local peoples had their own stories of how things came to be. A lot of times these stories were not in agreement with each other; the Cretans claimed their land as the birthplace of Zeus, but so did the Arcadians, and the Lydians, and the Dodonans as well. Who wouldn't want to lay claim to the King of Gods? With no one source, or one bible to record them, these stories were passed down through countless ages by bards, men who told the memorized stories of the Olympians.

Some of them eventually wrote down their stories, or had them transcribed, and this is how we know the names of Homer, of Hesiod, of Apollodoros. Each of these tellers, as did each of the tellers before them, added a little something of their own to the telling.

In *my* retellings of these stories, as the original superhero stories, I went as far back to the original sources as I could. There are many great retellings of the Greek myths available (I even recommend some elsewhere in this book) but I avoided the versions of other modern storytellers. Also, as I added my own twists here and there, I made connections that were not so apparent before and condensed a couple of characters into one, all in the interest of creating a whole tapestry of Greek mythology. I hope you enjoyed reading this story as much as I have enjoyed creating it.

George O'Connor
Brooklyn, NY
2009

A BRIEF NOTE ON NAMES

Some readers may notice that the names of some of the characters in Olympians are spelled differently than they may remember, for example Ouranos instead of Uranus, or Kronos instead of Cronus. This is because, whenever possible, I have tried to use the more "Greek" transliterations of their names, rather than the more familiar Latinized versions.

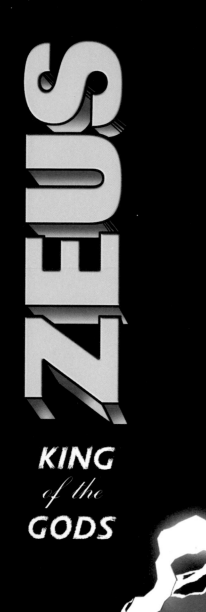

ZEUS

KING *of the* GODS

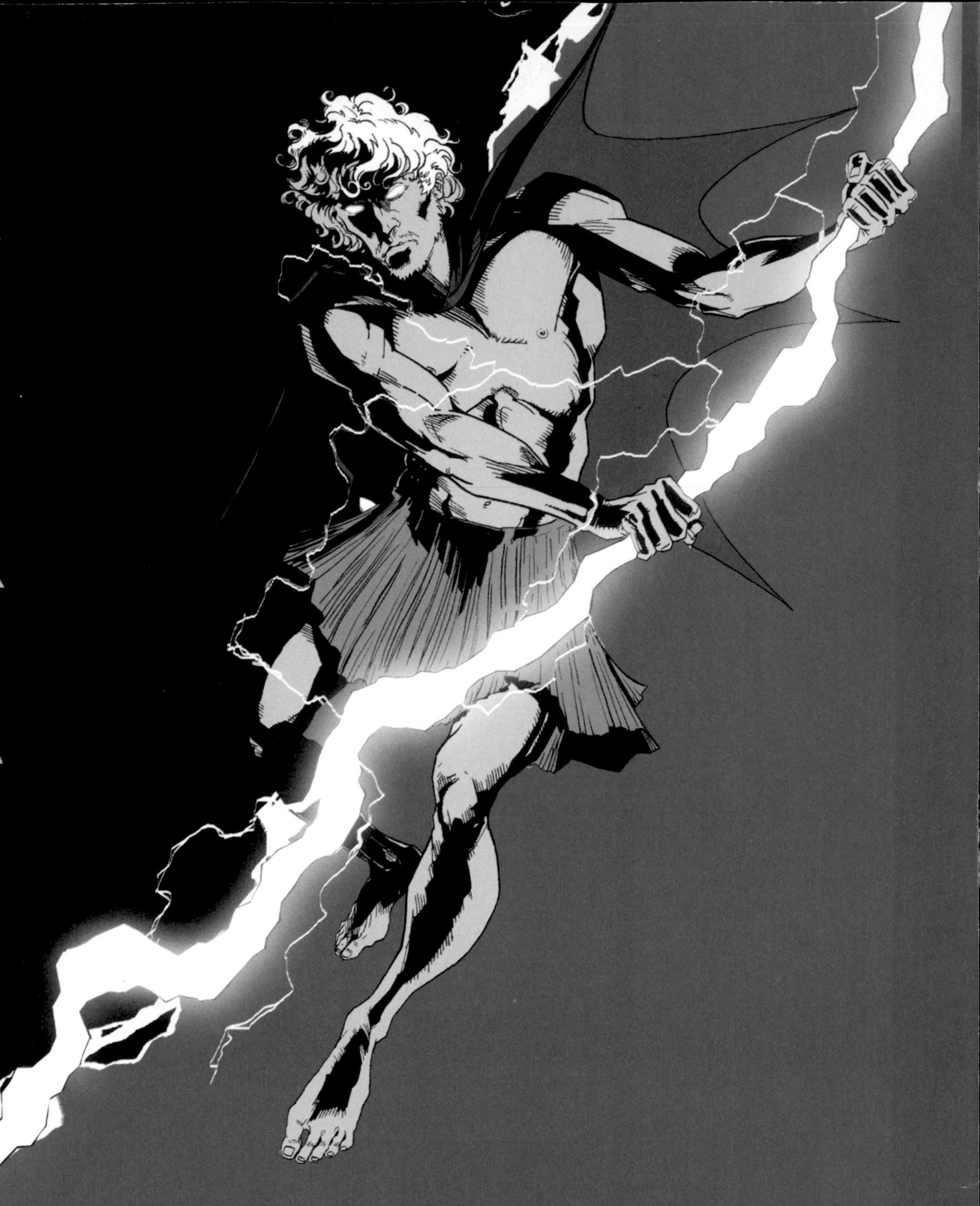

GOD OF the Sky, Storms, Thunder and Lightning, Justice, the Universe

ROMAN NAMES Jove, Jupiter

SYMBOL Lightning Bolt

SACRED ANIMAL Eagle

SACRED PLANT Oak

SACRED PLACES Mount Ida, Crete (place of birth), Olympia (site of the Olympic festival games), Dodona (location of Zeus' oracle), Mount Olympus (home of the Olympian gods)

DAY OF THE WEEK Thursday

PLANET Jupiter

MODERN LEGACY The eagle, as symbol of the United States, can be traced back to the sacred symbol of Zeus. The Olympic games began in ancient Greece, as a festival held every four year to honor Zeus

GREEK NOTES

PAGE 4-5, PANEL 2: The Titans are: Kronos, Oceanus, Iapetus, Hyperion, Krios, and Polos; the Titanesses are Rhea, Tethys, Theia, Phoebe, Themis and Mnemosyne.

PAGE 4-5, PANEL 3: The word "cyclopes" translates as "round eye."

PAGE 4-5, PANEL 4: "Hekatonchieres" means "hundred-handed." The three hekatonchieres were named Briareos ("strong, stout"), Kottos ("Grudge") and Gyes ("Of the Land").

PAGE 4-5, PANEL 5: According to Hesiod, Tartaros is so far beneath the surface of the Earth that if you were to drop an anvil from the surface, it would take nine days to reach Tartaros!

PAGE 4-5, PANEL 7: Adamantine is the nigh-unbreakable substance that Gaea used to fashion Kronos's sickle. The comic book character Wolverine, of the X-Men, has a skeleton and claws laced with an almost unbreakable metal called adamantium, which takes its name from this substance.

PAGE 6, PANELS 1-4: Hyperion ("he who watches from above") was situated in the east, associated as he was with the Sun and Moon (he's their father, after all), which both rise in the East. Iapetus ("the piercer") was the farthest from Hyperion's light, which placed him in the West. Polos, the northern Titan, had a name that literally meant "pole," as in the north pole. Krios ("ram") was in the south; he is associated with the goat constellation Aries, which rises from the south.

PAGE 6, PANEL 5: Can you guess which familiar modern-day word we get from Oceanus?

PAGE 7, PANEL 1: Kronos's name means, simply, time. His habit of eating people comes from the fact that everything, from animals to people to stones to even gods, eventually get worn away, or eaten, by time.

PAGE 8, PANEL 2: The Gigantes' name translates as "The Earth-born." We still use words such as "giant" or "gigantic" to describe something huge, an idea derived from the Gigantes. Watch for more of them in Book Two of Olympians—*Athena: The Grey-Eyed Goddess*.

PAGE 8, PANEL 3: The nymphs, whose name translates as "young women," were not immortal, like the gods, but rather were extremely long lived.

PAGE 8, PANEL 4: The Furies were also known as the Erinyes, and the Fates were known as the Moirae.

PAGE 8, PANEL 5: Here's a hint: it's about Aphrodite.

PAGE 10, PANEL 3: It was not unheard of in the ancient world for Mother Earth to give prophecies through cracks in her surface, such as the famous oracle at Delphi.

PAGE 12, PANEL 4: Nectar was the drink and ambrosia was the food of the gods. The horn of Amalthea, the cornucopia, or horn of plenty, is a symbol still in use today.

PAGE 13, PANEL 4: Prometheus means forethought; Epimetheus means afterthought.

PAGE 23, PANEL 5: Balanis, the nymph of the trees pictured here, has a name that translates as "Acorn tree."

PAGE 24, PANEL 2: Polybotes the Gigante has a name that translates as "feeding many." No wonder he got the job of bringing food to Kronos the all-devouring. Polybotes eventually meets his end in the war of the Gigantes, when Poseidon throws an entire island on top of him!

PAGE 24, PANEL 7: The name Zeus takes here, of Kelmis, was the name of one of the shield-clanging nymphs, or couretes, who guarded him in his cave when he was an infant.

PAGE 27, PANEL 5: The actual stone that Kronos coughed up was venerated at the oracle in Delphi. They called it the omphalos, or belly button, because it was thought to be at the center of the world.

PAGES 28, 29: There is a little hint here of what each of the newly released Olympians will become the god of in where they land. Poseidon falls into the sea, Hades smashes into the Earth, and Demeter lands in a field of grain. Hestia, goddess of the hearth and the least developed of the Olympians, is depicted as a flickering flame. Hera, who is a goddess of the air and sky, never falls to earth at all—rather she is lowered carefully in the arms of her future husband, Zeus.

PAGE 34, PANEL 3: That's Prometheus, always a champion to mankind, herding mortals into a cave to protect them from the Titan's wrath.

PAGE 34, PANEL 4: Here are some of the Olympians, taking the forms of what would become their sacred animals. The eagle is Zeus, the panther is Hera, the snake is Demeter, and the horse is Poseidon.

PAGE 38: Kampe the dragon's name means "crooked" or "winding," like the path to Tartaros itself.

PAGE 41, PANEL 5: The gates to Tartaros were made of Adamantine, the same material as Kronos's sickle.

PAGE 50, PANEL 3: The Cyclopes were master craftsmen and, upon being freed by Zeus, they presented him with his thunderbolt, Poseidon with his earthquake-causing trident, and Hades with his helmet of invisibility.

PAGE 61, PANEL 5: Where indeed? That's another tale for another day...

PAGE 64, PANEL 1: The Greeks viewed the rule of Kronos as being the Golden Age, when people's needs were met; however they had no art, society, or culture. The light of the new age that is pouring through the tattered sky is the beginning of the Silver Age, the age of civilization. The ancient Greeks whose stories I am adapting believed they were living at the end of the Iron Age, after the Silver and Bronze Ages.

PAGE 65, PANEL 2: The image of Atlas holding up the sky (or sometimes, the globe) is a very familiar one today. Among many other things, the Atlantic Ocean takes its name from Atlas.

PAGE 66, PANEL 1: Can you name them all? Clockwise, from top left are Zeus, Hera, Demeter, Ares (Hades in shadow, behind him), Aphrodite, Hephaistos, Dionysos, Artemis, Apollo, and Poseidon. In the center are Athena, Hermes, and Hestia. Don't worry if you don't know them all—you'll get to meet the rest of the Olympians in *Athena: Grey-Eyed Goddess*.

The CYCLOPES

ONE-EYED GIANTS

INDIVIDUAL NAMES	Brontes ("Thunder"), Steropes ("Lightning"), and Arges ("Flash")
GODS OF	Storms
NAME TRANSLATION	"Round Eye"
SACRED PLACES	Mount Etna, Sicily (site of the volcanic workshops they shared with Zeus's son, Hephaistos); Tiryns, Mycenae (sites of ancient stone walls believed to be built by the Cyclopes)
MODERN LEGACY	The name Cyclops is still widely used to describe a one-eyed monster. The leader of the comic-book superheroes the X-Men takes his name from these giants

ABOUT THIS BOOK

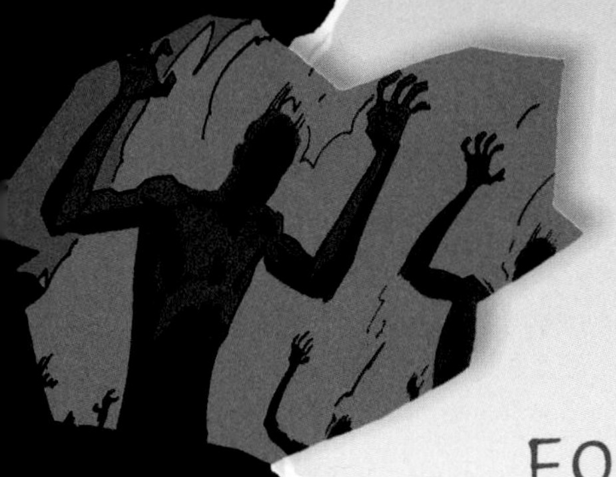

ZEUS: KING OF THE GODS is the first book in Olympians, a new graphic novel series from First Second that retells the Greek myths. This book is the story of how the ancient Greeks believed the world came into being, as well as the childhood and ascendancy of Zeus, who became the King of the Gods.

FOR DISCUSSION

1. Zeus's dad tries to eat him. Has your dad ever tried to eat you?

2. A lot of the names in this book will sound familiar; for example, Zeus' grandfather, Ouranos, has a name similar to Uranus, the planet. What other things can you think of that have similar names to characters in Greek mythology?

3. A lot of things that happened to Zeus may seem similar to other stories that you have heard—for instance, Zeus fighting against his evil father is like Luke Skywalker fighting against Darth Vader. What other stories do you know that are similar to what Zeus went through?

4. In many ways, Zeus and the other characters are like superheroes. What superheroes can you think of that are similar to characters in Greek mythology?

5. Kronos is a god of time, and he is described as devouring everything. Why do you think that is?

6. There were originally twelve Titans, and later there would be twelve Olympians. Why do you think that the number twelve was so important? What other numbers seem to be important in the Greek myths? Where else in the world do you see these numbers?

7. Very few people believe in the Greek gods today. Why do you think it is important that we still learn about them?

METIS

THE OCEAN'S DAUGHTER

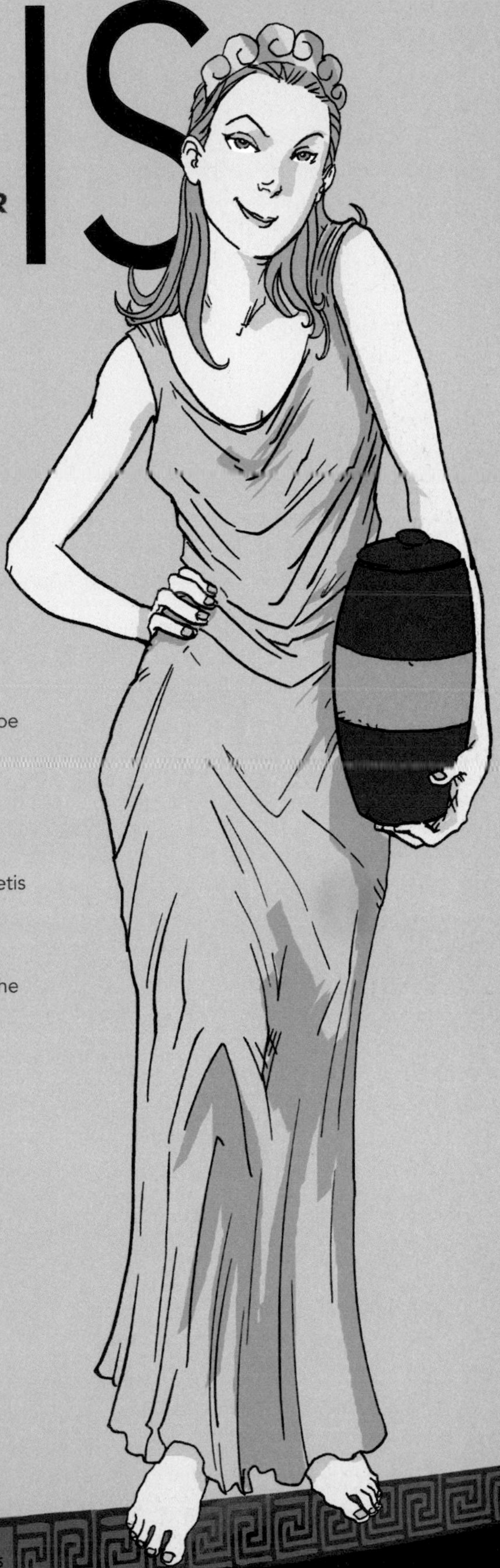

GODDESS OF Cunning, Good Advice, Planning

SACRED PLACES The ocean, Libya (believed by some to be the site of her daughter Athena's birth)

DAY OF THE WEEK Wednesday, a day she shared with Zeus's son, Hermes

PLANET Metis, a minor moon of Jupiter; Also Metis 9, a large asteroid between the planets Mars and Jupiter

MODERN LEGACY Metis's greatest modern legacy is that she is the mother of Athena, one of the greatest Olympians

BIBLIOGRAPHY

HESIOD: VOLUME 1, THEOGENY. WORKS AND DAYS: TESTIMONIA. HESIOD. NEW YORK: LOEB CLASSICAL LIBRARY, 2007.

Zeus: King of the Gods is unusual for this series because it takes the bulk of its inspiration from one source myth, Hesiod's *Theogony*, with a few little bits from other old myths sprinkled here and there.
The above is the copy I have in my personal collection; it was the best translation I found.

THEOI GREEK MYTHOLOGY WEBSITE WWW.THEOI.COM

Without a doubt, the single most valuable resource I came across in this entire venture. At theoi.com, you can find an encyclopedia of various gods and goddesses from Greek mythology, cross referenced with every mention of them they could find in literally hundreds of ancient Greek and Roman texts.

WWW.LIBRARY.THEOI.COM

A subsection of the above site, it's an online archive of hundreds of ancient Greek and Roman texts. Many of these have never been published in the traditional sense, and many are just fragments recovered from ancient papyrus, or recovered text from other authors' quotations of lost epics. Invaluable.

MYTH INDEX WEBSITE WWW.MYTHINDEX.COM

It seems this website is connected in some way to Theoi.com, and is still being updated, which is nice. While it doesn't have the painstakingly compiled quotations of ancient texts, it does offer some terrific encyclopedic entries of virtually every character to ever pass through a Greek myth. Pretty amazing.

ALSO RECOMMENDED
FOR YOUNGER READERS

The Gods and Goddesses of Olympus. Aliki. New York: HarperCollins, 1997.

D'Aulaires' Book of Greek Myths. Ingri and Edgar Parin D'Aulaire. New York: Doubleday, 1962.

Black Ships Before Troy. Rosemary Sutcliff and Alan Lee. London: Francis Lincoln, 2005.

Wanderings of Odysseus. Rosemary Sutcliff and Alan Lee. London: Francis Lincoln, 2005.

Z is for Zeus: A Greek Mythology Alphabet. Helen L. Wilbur and Victor Juhasz. Chelsea MI: Sleeping Bear Press, 2008.

FOR OLDER READERS

The Marriage of Cadmus and Harmony. Robert Calasso. New York: Knopf, 1993.

Mythology. Edith Hamilton. Madison WI: Demco, 1999.

Zeus: A Journey Through Greece in the Footsteps of a God. Tom Stone. New York: Bloomsbury USA, 2008.